CHRISTMAS INN LOVE

KELLY COLLINS

GET A FREE BOOK.

Go to www.authorkellycollins.com

CHAPTER ONE

CELIA

C elia Roberts pored over the books of the Hummingbird Inn. What made her think it was a great idea to operate an inn in a town that had seen better days?

Pinetop, Colorado was no Aspen, and it wasn't Vail. It barely registered on the map, but it was home.

Trying to make ends meet in a less than ideal economy could make a stronger woman weep. As she always did, when things looked bleak, she made a gratitude list and counted her blessings.

Jackson was healthy.

She could pay this month's bills.

They had food on the table.

It could be worse.

The fall sun filtered through her sheers and baked the desk.

The wind whipped around in sudden gusts like something big was about to blow in. It knocked the branches of an ancient apple tree against the house, mimicking the sound of someone knocking at the door. It had fooled her a couple of times until she learned to ignore it.

The knocking grew louder, and the cadence grew even and measured. This was not her apple tree.

She let go of her pen and walked through her living quarters into the inn toward the front door. Back when the property was a rustic retreat for an old-time Hollywood producer, her place served as the live-in help's quarters. It was funny to own a house but never live in the main part of it.

Today's visitor was unexpected. Her hands came up to straighten her messy bun. Strands escaped to frame her face. She wore no makeup and wasn't positive she'd washed her face that morning.

The day had started in a blur. She'd flown out of bed when her alarm hadn't gone off, worried that Jackson didn't get up for school. She'd found him downstairs devouring a box of Corn Flakes.

Her clothes were an afterthought. She wore an apron wrapped around her waist. Hidden underneath were old jeans, a faded T-shirt, and a pair of old Keds with the big toe worn through.

She peered through the side window and pressed her eyes tight to focus. It was just her luck she looked like a charity case while a nicely dressed, handsome man stood on her doorstep.

She considered turning around and ignoring the caller but reminded herself she needed whatever revenue she could muster. She wasn't prepared, nor in the mood to pretend she was happy about the unexpected visitor, but she counted to three, took a deep breath and opened the door.

"Hello, welcome to Hummingbird Inn." She painted on a happy-to-see-you smile.

The man glanced left and right before stepping inside. As he brushed past her, he didn't look in her eyes. He looked past her. Through her. His focus was on everything else, like he was sizing up the place.

She did the same, except her eyes made it back to him, and she couldn't stop staring. Holy hell, he was a fashion layout come to life. Centerfold or front-page worthy.

"Can I help you?" she asked.

He looked at her for the first time.

His face was familiar. She knew him from somewhere but couldn't make the connection.

"I'm looking for Celia, the owner." His voice was stern and unforgiving. Not the tone folks in Pinetop used when communicating with one another. Not the tone a friendly person used to greet someone. This man was not a friend but a foe.

"Celia?"

"Yes." He rubbed his jaw and leaned down like he was sharing a secret. "I hate to bother. Never thought I'd be in Pinetop again. You could say this is an unexpected and undesired reunion."

"Really? You don't like her?"

"I'm ambivalent. I knew her in high school." He lifted his shoulders. "It is what it is."

"I see," she said, checking him out. She had been popular back then and knew just about everyone, but she couldn't place him. Mr. Tall, Dark and Sexy would have left an impression for sure.

"One moment. I'll be back with her."

Celia offered him a seat in the parlor, which was the common area for guests. She dashed back to her quarters, working the hair tie out of her messy bun as she raced to her bathroom.

She slipped off her apron and hung it on the hook of the bathroom door. This man claimed to know her, and he didn't appear to like her. When she returned dressed like the inn owner instead of a homeless woman, he'd be surprised. Her T-shirt hit the floor along with her jeans. A clean and ironed button-down blouse paired with a tailored sports jacket, and slacks acted like armor.

She ran a brush through her hair, lined her eyes quickly with a soft brown, and colored her lips with a pale pink gloss. Her transformation was instant and boosted her confidence. No doubt it would surprise this man who knew her back in high school.

"Ambivalent. He sounds like he hated me," she murmured. "I was a damn saint back then."

She looked back at the mirror and touched her face. Had she changed so much to be unrecognizable now? Funny what years of unhappiness could do to a girl.

The clickety-clack of her heels on the wooden floor was the only warning he'd get. She found him focused on his cell phone, oblivious to her arrival. She cleared her throat. He glanced at her casually and then returned to his call.

She knew the exact moment he figured her out.

He froze, and in slow motion he lifted his head.

"Hi," she said in her most pleasant voice. "Celia Roberts, the girl from high school. Pleased to meet you." She relished his stunned expression as she shook his hand. "I'm afraid I don't remember you. You are?" she asked with a slight bite to her voice.

"I'm Robert McKenna," he said.

"Bobby McKenna," she repeated with surprise. "Little Bobby McKenna? No way!"

His eyes rolled back as his face tipped toward the ceiling. "No one has called me that for a while."

Back in high school, the jocks, including the guy who would become her ex-husband, got in trouble teasing the freshmen. Bobby McKenna hadn't been a freshman, but he was small for his age and got caught in their bullying.

"You grew up." She took him in from the top of his lush brown hair to the tips of his Italian loafers.

Six feet looked good on him. Sculpted cheekbones, a strong jaw, and eyes the color of a spring sky made Bobby a hand-some man. He'd been a cute kid but had the worst knack for attracting attention. For whatever reason, the guys in her crowd never let up.

"Yes," he said. "Not that you would have noticed, but I hit six feet before I graduated. I go by Rob now."

She gawked at him. There was no way he'd looked like this in high school. She would have remembered. The face in front of her was not one she could easily forget. This Bobby was remarkable.

She shook those thoughts from her head. "What can I do for you?"

"I'm not here to ask a favor."

"Then what brings you to my doorstep? Do you need a room?" His mother had passed away a few months ago. There was no mention of a memorial service. Fiona McKenna simply disappeared.

Instead of answering her question, he asked a different one.

"Why didn't you tell me who you were?"

"You mean when you were telling me how unlikable I was?"

He didn't bother to acknowledge her response.

"You could have told me right away." He looked at her like she was a piece of home-made pie. Flaky crust and just out of the oven.

"You didn't give me a chance." She squared her shoulders and stood tall. "You insulted me the first opportunity you got."

"You didn't identify yourself."

Her balled fists dug into her hips. This might not be a fight she could win, but it wasn't one she'd back down from without an apology. "You made assumptions, and you weren't nice."

His expression softened to weary acceptance. "You're right. I apologize."

If he wasn't so pleasant to look at, would she have already shown him the door? In times like these, it was important to remember her gratitude list. Her ex-husband made her sensitive to criticism, especially when it came from men.

"Mr. McKenna, why are you at the Hummingbird Inn? Can I get you a room?" She wasn't in the mood to take his attitude, but she'd happily take his money.

He shook his head. "No."

"Well then, I have lots to do and little time to do it. Indulge me. Why are you here?"

"I'm getting there.' He walked around the parlor. "Your property borders mine."

"My property isn't near anything." She looked out the window, expecting to find something other than the land that had been empty for years. "On one side is another house like this one and on the other side is a creek and acres of wilderness. I know who owns the house next door, and it's not you."

"Nope. You're right." He cocked his head. "I own the wilderness. Or my mother did until she passed away. I put up a house on the far end of the property where I'm living now."

"I'm familiar with your mother. I think I would have known if Fiona owned the land next to mine." Was it possible for every blood cell in her body to migrate to her head? Ready to burst, she took several calming breaths. "You must be mistaken."

Rob stepped forward, moving so close his cologne tickled her nose.

"I'm not wrong," he said. "She had her place in town where I grew up, but this land has been in our family forever. She didn't want to sell it because she wanted to keep it in the family, or so I assume."

"You built a new house when she had a perfectly good one for you to live in?" She dropped her hands and walked to the fireplace mantel, where she rearranged the figurines several times.

"I wouldn't say it's perfectly good. It's old and poorly maintained. As for my house, I've honored the spirit of the town by building a Victorian, instead of going with the modern structure I had pictured in my mind. At least that's what it appears to be on the outside. Inside it's a modern marvel." He shrugged his broad shoulders. "Anyway, I'm here to let you know I have plans for the property which will drastically change the approach to your place and mine."

"Speak English." She glared at him.

"I own all the land behind you, and I'm developing it."

"Developing it how?" Her hand went to her chest as she felt her heart sink. Development was another word for change, and she didn't like change.

"My vision is a resort village with cabins and a golf course. I'm exploring snowmaking capabilities, so skiing may be an option."

"You're kidding, right?" She breathed deeply, not willing to give in to the anger building inside of her. "Skiing? You just dropped by to let me know you're putting a recreational urban sprawl next door to my business? Mr. McKenna, I make my living off cozy and quaint. I'm raising my son on small-town values. What is phase two of your plan? To import gangs?"

He walked over and lowered himself enough to make them eye to eye. Looking into those baby blues made it hard to concentrate. *Focus, you're a professional.*

"I'm not importing gangs, but I'll refer to my business plan to see if it was a consideration. I'm a business developer. This is what I do. I've come home to add value to the land so I can sell it. This property has been sitting undeveloped forever. It's time to bring Pinetop into this century."

"Pinetop is developed. Has been for over a hundred years. It has everything a person could need or want."

Being near him took the gnash out of her bite.

"It has everything except a decent economy, good entertainment, and edible food." His list was small but accurate.

"It went as far as it could go, Mr. McKenna," she responded. "And the food at the counter is fabulous."

"Rob," he corrected. "Does Myrtle still make a mean meatloaf sandwich?"

How had the conversation turned from destroying her livelihood to eating at the drugstore counter? "Everything Myrtle makes is noteworthy."

"Good to know, but Pinetop could offer more." He smiled and her insides twisted. Surely it was agitation and not attraction that had her heart skipping a beat and her stomach dropping to her black leather pumps.

"If there was something more than what we offer, it would have been here by now. That means you can't turn Pinetop into Aspen no matter how much you tear up the ground. That's business 101 or at the most 102."

"Wharton Business School?" he asked sarcastically.

"No, Pinetop School of Hard Knocks. Graduated with honors." There was enough ice in her voice to drop the inside temperature by ten degrees. "I put my heart and soul into my business, and I'm not giving it up."

"I'm not asking you to, Ms. Roberts, but heart and soul have no place in business. Emotions don't pay the rent, keep the lights on, or put food on the table. That's lesson numero uno in any business school."

"If changing Pinetop was what Fiona wanted, she would have sold the land long ago. It appears she wanted you to keep it."

"She asked me to use my best judgment, and I believe I have." He produced a business card and walked toward the door, where he tucked it under the fancy rotary dial telephone on the entryway table. "Call me if you have questions."

She held up her hand. "I've got one."

He turned around. "I'm all ears."

"When will you be leaving?"

"Not until I have everything I want." He looked at her as if she was also on his menu.

A shiver raced through her, but it wasn't unpleasant. She was torn between wanting to clobber the man and wanting to kiss him.

CHAPTER TWO

ROB

Rob McKenna was back in his hometown for one purpose and one purpose only, to pounce on the opportunity in Pinetop.

He sipped a diet soda and looked out the wall of glass that showcased the wilderness behind his new prefab home.

He had no previous plan of attack for the three hundred acres his mother left him. He'd never considered the land because right after high school graduation, he left home to make his way in the world. Now, he couldn't resist the prospect the land presented to a man like him—a property developer. It was the first time he'd considered business where emotional loose ends were part of the package.

He freely admitted that when he knew he was coming back home, the first thought he'd had was of Celia Roberts. There was a real possibility she wouldn't be in Pinetop, but fortunately for him, she was. Why he hadn't noticed her was a mystery. Was it because her hair was shorter and darker? Gone was the girl with the sparkle in her eye and in her place was a woman who looked as if life had not been all that kind. She was still beautiful, but the ethereal light that once shined from her was gone.

He thought the experience of his hometown would be different now that he was a grown man with an impressive portfolio, but it wasn't. The old town had been spit-polished to show its quaintness and charm, but it conjured demons he thought were long gone. They churned in his stomach as he took in the acreage in front of him.

When he returned after his mother's funeral, he knew he would be here for a while. While it would have been nice to snap his fingers and have the place transform, development didn't happen that way. Even the kind of development he did took time. He needed a place to stay and his mother's house would never do. Every wall held the voices of contempt and disappointment. That's why he'd contracted to set a Victorian style modular home on the edge of his family's property closest to Pinetop town limits. It might be a home now, but he would convert it to the business center later. He shipped everything he owned from back east, including his sports car. There were some luxuries he refused to do without, and a fast car was one of them.

A soft tap on the front door grabbed his attention. He powered across the wooden floors and swung the door open to reveal the first visitor he'd received at the new place. It was an older man with a blunt shaved haircut and pants stained with the memory of manual labor.

"Morning." He lowered his eyes to take in the big dog tethered by a leash wrapped around the old man's gnarled hands. He wasn't an expert on animals but thought this might be a golden retriever.

Rob was about to let the fellow in, but he wasn't familiar with the animal.

"Can I help you?" He looked between the dog and the man.

"I'm Dave Swanson, a friend of your mother's. I'm sorry for your loss." He bowed his head, but his gravelly voice split the air. "I wrote you about taking care of her dog." He looked at the beast who danced beside him and let out a stern, "Sit." The pup obediently sat and leaned against Dave's leg. "She only had the fella for the last half a year before she passed, and I've had him ever since." He ruffled the dog's fur. "Lucky is a good pup."

"Glad to hear it, and you're here why?" He had to admit the dog drew him in. He had a sweet face and appeared obedient.

"You said you would take the dog once you were in town." He looked beyond him to the interior of the house.

"I did?" He had no recollection of speaking to the man.

"Your secretary or somebody at your office said you'd be happy to take him since he belonged to your mom. She sent me all the information so I could find you." He stepped back and looked at the house. "I got the right address. The construction was finished, so I thought I'd see if you were here. Lucky me." He looked down at the dog. "Or lucky Lucky."

Rob laughed. If he hadn't moved his operation to his new home, he would let his secretary go all over again. Something told him his lack of information was Pam's retribution.

There was something likable about the man and the dog, and he couldn't bring himself to tell him no as much as he wanted to.

"Won't you come in, Mr. Swanson?" He stepped aside to give them room. "What's the dog's name again?"

"Lucky," said Dave. "And so far, he has been."

"So it seems." Rob looked around his house. It wasn't built for active animals with its wood floors and light carpet. "Unfortunately, my secretary did not pass on the message to me, and I'm not set up for a dog."

"He's no problem. Short of a few temporary lapses of judgment, times where his puppy brain takes over, Lucky is well-trained. Keep him close," he said. "He's socialized and used to going into town. You can buy everything from dog food to chews at Pinetop Grocer. They don't mind if he comes in the store. Everyone there knows him." He looked at the leash in his hand. "If you drive to the new shopping center outside of town, that's a different story. They're not so animal friendly."

"Thank you, Mr. Swanson," he said. "I guess we'll figure it out."

"It's Dave."

"My name is Rob." He offered his hand to shake. "Is there something else? Can I offer you a drink?"

Dave shuffled his feet and looked at the ground. "Your assistant said you would gladly reimburse me for caring for him." He pulled a folded piece of paper from his pocket and thrust it forward. "This is what I've paid to keep him happy since your mom's passing."

"No problem." Rob skimmed the numbers until he got to the bottom line, which was less than he paid for a nice dinner in the city.

"I'm on a fixed income or I wouldn't ask. I moved in next to your mom when my mother passed on a few years ago. The place needed a lot of work and I've put my last dime in nails and paint."

That explained his well-worn clothes. "You're Roberta's son?"

"Yes, sir. Didn't grow up here like you did, but I fell in love with Pinetop the first time I visited."

Rob had never been enamored with the town. A person would miss it if they blinked their eye at the right time.

"Will a check do?"

"Yeah, a check is fine."

He didn't mind that his assistant had spoken on his behalf. Dave was kind to keep his mother's dog. He walked over to his desk and pulled out his checkbook. His pen sailed across the paper and he ripped off the check, which included a sizable bonus.

"There you go," he said. "Thanks for taking care of him."

Dave handed him the leash and Lucky happily walked to his new owner.

Rob wasn't ready to be responsible for anyone or anything. He'd just come to terms with losing his mother out of the blue. She hadn't been sick. According to everyone, Fiona McKenna had been healthy until that night she laid her head on the pillow and didn't wake up. He always thought she'd outlive him because she was too ornery to die. Even now, her voice lived in his head, and it told him he better take care of her friend Dave.

He looked at the older man in front of him. "Can I give you a ride somewhere?"

"I drove."

"Let me walk you out." He glanced at the dog who looked up at him like he hung the moon. "It looks like Lucky and I have some shopping to do."

He should have considered his mom had a pet. She'd gone through a few since he'd left town. They acted as substitute children who didn't talk back.

Rob hit the garage door opener on their way out and revealed his two-seater Jaguar. Both men stood blinking at the sports car as the dilemma became obvious. It wasn't designed for animal transport.

"On second thought"—Rob pulled out his phone—"I'll see if the store will deliver."

Dave let go of a belly laugh. "Good luck with that," he said as he climbed into his truck.

Maybe I should pick up a truck while I'm in town.

He led the dog back into the house and searched the internet for the telephone number of Pinetop Grocer. It took some doing, but he eventually persuaded the manager with the help of a hundred-dollar delivery fee to let a stock boy bring out an order. Until then, they'd wait.

Seeing Lucky sit at the back door looking like he needed to go out compelled him to open the French doors. The problem was he had no fence. The dog tore out the back like he'd been shot from a pistol.

Rob burst across the threshold after him, shouting his name as though it would get the desired result, and Lucky would return.

He was frantic, hoping the dog would head back to the house. Rob didn't know what he'd do if he ran into the thick brush beyond.

A young man leaned against a beat-up Ford pickup parked in his drive. The kid took in the scene in front of him. Tall and lanky, his thick hair fell across his eyes. With a clap of his hands and a whistle, Lucky switched direction and headed straight to him.

"Hey, boy. How are you doing?"

Lucky's entire back end wagged.

Rob halted in his tracks, knowing a teenager and a dog had outsmarted him.

"Pinetop Grocer?" asked Rob.

"Yep. I set your order on the porch."

Rob checked the boy's name tag. *Jackson.*

The only other Jackson he knew in Pinetop was Jackson Westbrook, who'd once held him by his ankles over a garbage can full of grass clippings. He saw no resemblance between this Jackson and that one, except for the height. But when the kid lifted his head and swept the hair out of his eyes, the face was recognizable. *Celia.*

"This is a random question, but is your mother Celia Roberts, by any chance?"

"Yes," Jackson replied casually.

"You're Jackson Westbrook?"

The boy looked at him like he was from the moon.

"No," he replied in a pensive tone. "I'm Jackson Roberts."

The dog rubbed against Jackson's hand as if begging for attention. The two of them appeared to hit it off.

"I'm an old friend of your mother's, and I recently moved back into town. You have your mother's eyes." Rob pulled out a hundred dollars from his wallet and offered it to him. "Thanks for making the delivery."

"Oh, no," Jackson said. "Mr. Starr from the store said you paid by credit card."

"This is for you." Rob saw immediately that Jackson had two things he needed. He drove a truck, and he was good with the dog. The healthy tip might benefit him in the long run. "What do they pay you at the grocery store?"

He stared at the Benjamin Franklin. "I make twelve an hour." Jackson shoved his hands into his pockets like he didn't trust himself to not grab the large bill.

"I inherited this dog from my mother—" he began.

"Lucky," Jackson said. "I know. I knew your mother. Lucky was always at the store with her."

"I've been told." Rob wasn't allowed to have a pet as a child. Was it fate's cruel joke to give him one now when he wasn't prepared?

"She brought him everywhere with her. Same as the last dog she had. That's how I remember her. She always had a dog with her," he said, fluffing Lucky's thick fur.

Rob had a good mind just to give the boy the dog.

"I don't suppose your mother would let you have him, would she? I mean since you're so good with him and all."

Jackson shook his head and laughed. "I don't think so."

Sending him home with Lucky would be a mean joke to play on Celia. No doubt he owed her something for all those years she'd stood by and watched the torture.

"In that case, I need some help. Do you think you or someone you know could come by and walk him until I get a fence put up? I'll pay twenty-five bucks a walk."

Jackson blinked with disbelief. "That's way too much to walk a dog."

Rob had no idea what the going rate was, but in his experience overpaying always brought out volunteers. "I figure you'd have to drive out here, so that's gas and wear and tear on your truck. Then there's your time. I was thinking every other day, either morning or afternoon would work, and I'll cover the rest. It would be somewhere in the neighborhood of a hundred a week?"

"Are you rich, mister?"

"I'm comfortable," he answered. "Think it over and let me know." He reached for Lucky's collar. "Thanks for bringing him back. I would have never caught him myself."

Jackson left and Rob took Lucky into the house. They passed the stack of pet supplies on his porch. Lucky looked up at him and seemed to smile.

"You're a troublemaker. Now I have to find a contractor to put up a fence." He put the dog in a guest room with a rawhide chew and left for the town hall and the permits department to find out what the rules were about erecting an enclosure for the dog. He also needed to get the ball rolling on developing the land.

He was almost to town when his phone rang. He didn't pay attention to the number or the name. He just answered.

"Rob McKenna."

"Celia Roberts," she replied.

He didn't think he'd hear from her again and couldn't say it made him unhappy.

"Ah, Mrs. Westbrook, to what do I owe the pleasure?"

"It's Roberts." Her voice was laced with displeasure. "You offered my son twenty-five bucks to walk a dog?"

"Yes," he said. "I inherited my mother's dog, and I'm not good with him. Your son apparently has the knack."

"My son already has a job." Her voice rose to levels that could cause hearing impairment.

"Okay." Something about thinking of her as a mother touched him. "I thought I was offering him an opportunity since I need help with the dog. Your son seemed to make Lucky happy, and vice versa. I respect your decision. I won't ask again."

"Wait—" she said. "He can do it as long as he keeps his grades up. If he wants to do it, I don't care. What exactly do you expect from him for twenty-five dollars?"

"I'm not asking for a kidney. Only to walk the furry beast a couple times a week. I'll walk him as well, but there will be days I can't. I'll only need him until I get a fence."

"Where is your house?" she asked. "It's not on my end of your property."

"No," he said. "The approach is from the other side. I get amazing sun most of the day."

"Oh, that's right. You built a Victorian knock-off."

Rob laughed softly. "I'm surprised there wasn't talk around town about the new house being built."

"The town is focused on other things, Mr. McKenna."

"What would those be?"

Something about her captivated him. He would have to remind her to stop calling him Mr. McKenna, but in truth, he liked the way it rolled off her tongue.

"Just the usual small-town stuff." Her tone was the type that came with an eye roll. "Nothing you'd be interested in. Since we'll be in the middle of your urban sprawl soon, this year will have to count."

"Why is that?" His project wouldn't hurt Pinetop. It would enhance the tiny town, bring infrastructure and innovation to a town that hadn't matured since the early nineteen hundreds.

"Never mind. You wouldn't understand."

"Help me understand."

She let out a breath that sounded half sigh and half growl. "We have two huge events at the end of the year. I mean, we have them throughout the year, but these are dear to my heart. There's the harvest festival and then we have our Christmas Parade. They're a big deal."

"I vaguely remember those growing up. I never could figure it out—"

"Couldn't figure out what?"

"Maybe you can tell me what the town harvests to celebrate?"

"I knew you wouldn't understand. I had this gut instinct it would be a mistake to share it with you, and I was right." The words came out like a slap of a ruler to his knuckles.

"No, no," he apologized. "I was teasing. It's a valid question but I—"

"Didn't mean to make fun? Yes, you did. I heard it in your voice. You feel superior. You'll shape up this area so it's worth something to you and you alone. I won't take back my approval of Jackson walking your dog as long as it makes him happy, but I'll warn him not to look up to you. He's vulnerable, and you're the kind of man he'd admire. If you hurt him or let him down, you'll answer to me." And with that, Celia ended the call.

Her words bothered him. It wasn't what she said, as much as what she didn't say. She gave him the distinct impression that Jackson had no father figure to speak of, which meant she was alone. Curiosity consumed him. What had happened to his onetime nemesis, Jackson Westbrook, Sr.?

He called her right back. The old Rob might have asked her flat out, but something held him back.

"Don't hang up," he blurted. "I apologize for hiring your son without your permission, and I'm sorry for casting a shadow on your holiday celebration." He was quiet, expecting she'd say something, but she didn't. "I hope we can talk about what my plans are. Would you like to come to my makeshift office and go over them? You and Jackson can both visit if you like. We'll have dinner—"

"Dinner at your office?" she asked.

"It's a home office."

"No, thanks."

"Okay then. Let's move on. I can count on Jackson tomorrow to walk the dog or is that a no too?"

"I already said it was fine."

"Then we have nothing else to talk about. That's a shame because I think I could enjoy talking to you." He hadn't meant to say that last part out loud, but it was too late.

"Goodbye, Mr. McKenna."

He parked his car and walked into the town hall building. While there, he checked out the death index on a hunch. He entered the name Jackson Westbrook, and nothing popped up. That was good, he thought. Jackson Sr. hadn't passed away, at least not locally.

He searched for the answer to his question. What had happened between them? He pulled up the court records online which were open to the public and entered Jackson's name. He got a hit. They'd divorced a decade ago. Rob opened the file. The grounds for the dissolution of marriage was abandonment. His heart twisted. The Jackson he knew was a guy who had everything in the world, including a beautiful family, and he'd chucked it away. That didn't sit well with him. Who in their right mind would toss Celia and Jackson Jr. aside?

After he finished playing amateur sleuth, he picked up the forms and documents he needed and introduced himself to the various key players in the permits department. He always had the ability to charm a crowd. He believed in the old adage about catching more flies with honey than vinegar.

Back in the car, he tossed the forms onto the passenger seat. His mind was not on business. After learning what he had, his head was full of thoughts about Celia, her son, and the drama he imagined they'd gone through. How bad had it been?

CHAPTER THREE

CELIA

Celia ended her call with Rob. Her face was hot, and her heart beat so hard she could feel it outside her chest. When Jackson announced he'd be paid all that money to walk a dog, she felt like a leaf spinning in the wind.

For so long, she had been in complete control. It was a thing she strived for, especially after her son was born and it was clear his father had major issues.

She needed to maintain stability for herself and Jackson and having someone breeze into town and take an interest in him rocked her boat. Her son needed male role models, but she wasn't certain Rob was the right man for that job. Then again, she wasn't sure he wasn't. Outside of the threat of taking her livelihood away, she had no qualms with the man.

Trust wasn't something she gave easily, but there was something about the sound of Rob's voice that she liked. It was crazy because he frustrated her as much as fascinated her. The boy had turned into a man. A successful, sexy man.

She shook those thoughts from her mind. His presence was no good for her. He had the ability to fracture an internal wall she had carefully constructed. It was a protective mechanism that let her be cheerful and interested on the outside but keep her vulnerability neatly in check.

That deep rumbling voice of his shook her foundation to its core. If he stayed in Pinetop too long, things could get dangerous. She had to remind herself about her priorities and her loneliness wasn't one of them.

Her mental gratitude list rose in her mind and she counted her blessings. Her son was healthy and strong and everything a young man his age ought to be. The inn made all its bills for the month, so she could breathe easily enough to relax and campaign for more business. While late spring was her best season because people liked to come out to the Old West, she would pitch holiday retreats, nonetheless.

Another plus was Celia had her health. That was important. If she didn't take care of herself, she couldn't be the best she knew how to be for her son. Add in that Pinetop was the best place to live, and her community was amazing, and she'd have to say she was fortunate.

After finishing her list of things to be grateful for, the pounding in her chest subsided, and she felt better.

Needing supplies that only Jackson's truck could carry, she dropped him off at work and headed toward the hardware store.

The citizens were preparing to build Christmas Parade floats for the holiday extravaganza scheduled only a few weeks away. They rehabbed the tops of previous floats with new themes to save money. Her task was to price out materials and pick things up if they were affordable.

To draw attention to the Hummingbird Inn, she had her own float this year but was sadly without inspiration. Nothing seemed to resonate. The town tried to stick with small-town values or the typical Christmas themes, but inspiration had evaded her.

She motored along until the engine of the old Ford sputtered. It ran like a well-oiled machine most of the time, but lately it had been making odd noises. A red light flashed on the truck's dashboard just as she hit her first stop sign toward town.

She didn't recognize the lit-up symbol and thought about the time she didn't put the gas cap on correctly and a similar light turned on in her car. Since she was so close to town, she figured she could make it to the gas station and have Mike take a look. She rolled forward, the truck coughed, and the light flashed again, making her rethink her strategy. *Practice what you preach. Safety first.*

She pulled onto the soft shoulder of the road and reached into the glove box for the manual. It wasn't her truck, and she didn't want to take any chances.

As she leafed through the pages, a car pulled up behind her. It was a fancy, low sitting sports car that reminded her of a shiny blue gemstone. She rolled her eyes when she saw the driver. She sat still as if by doing so, Rob wouldn't notice her.

"Hey, Jackson," he called out as he approached the driver's side door.

Tinting the windows was one of the first things her son had done when he bought the truck, like somehow that would make it hip.

She tried to set aside her anxiety at seeing him again. He stirred her in so many ways.

That he stopped to help touched her heart even though he was thinking it was Jackson who was in trouble. The fact that he thought it was Jackson affected her more. He showed more concern than his father ever had.

She rolled down the window and smiled. "I'm not Jackson."

"No, you're not," he said. "Is there trouble or did you just pull over?"

There was enough smolder in his voice to make her heart race.

She pointed to the dash. "A red light came on," She held up the manual. "I was looking it up."

He leaned on the door, his head peeking inside the window. "Turn her on, and let's have a look."

She did as he asked, all the while breathing in the scent of his cologne. It was light and spicy and filled her nose with amber and vanilla and a hint of cinnamon.

She turned the key, and the light flashed.

"Okay," he said. "You can turn her off. It's coolant. Hold on one second."

Rob leaned back and checked out the truck bed, then reached in and lifted a bottle.

"As I suspected," he said. "Jackson has a leak, and he's probably been doctoring it by filling up the well as needed."

"All I need is to put that in and I'll be good to go?" she asked enthusiastically.

"Not so fast," he said with a mild chuckle. "You're hot right now."

She blinked. "I am?" Her hand went to her hair to brush it from her eyes.

He raised his brows and smiled. "What I meant to say is the engine is hot. Let's let her sit a bit, and then you can put this in. Do you and Jackson share the truck?"

"It's his, but I borrow it." It was a harmless question and Celia gave up the answer easily. She was more guarded with strangers, but then again, Rob wasn't really a stranger. He was just a person she hadn't seen in a long time. In a small town, no one was actually a stranger.

"I just bought a truck myself. I'm having it delivered in a few days. Everyone around here seems to have one, and Lucky and I don't fit in my car."

"Lucky?"

"That's the dog."

She noted that his face was engaged in a mild smirk as he looked at her. She wasn't sure if he was mocking her somehow.

"Right ... the dog. Everyone in town knew Fiona's dog by sight. I didn't remember his name. Her owning all that land had to be the best kept secret in the world. I still can't get over it."

He nodded. "I think you can pop the hood now. I'm happy to cover the repair. I can follow you, and we can drop her off at a service station."

"I'll bet Jackson can fix this himself," she said. "Besides, I would want to ask him before I made any plans on his behalf. Part of growing up is being responsible for yourself."

"He's a good kid. I don't know him all that well, but sometimes you can tell these things." He pushed off the door and took a step back. "I offered the fix as a gift. It might be selfish, but if he can't drive his truck, he can't get to my place to walk the dog. I'll default to your motherly wisdom. Whatever you think is best."

First, the high wages for dog walking and now this. His generosity irked Celia, and she wasn't exactly sure why. She searched her feelings until she realized she didn't trust him. It wasn't him specifically, but men's motives in general.

For the longest time, she'd fantasized about a man who would be there for her and for Jackson, and in the slightest way, Rob was. Now she was pushing back. It all came down to her ex-husband who should have been there for both of them but wasn't.

"If you open the hood, I'll fill up the coolant. You should be able to make it into town and back to your place."

She popped the hood and spied through the opening it created. Bits of Rob, with his boyish disheveled hair and fleece-lined denim jacket, showed through the opening as he serviced her truck. She wouldn't have taken him for the type to know anything about cars, but then again, he was from Pinetop. You could take the man out of the country but couldn't take the country out of the man.

Rob closed the hood and gave it a pat. He walked to the truck bed and put the coolant back where he'd found it. He wiped his hands together and Celia instinctively reached for the glove box again.

"Here." She searched around and let out a sigh before she closed it up. "Sorry."

"What's up?"

She stopped. "I keep baby wipes in my car. Apparently, Jackson doesn't."

His smile dazzled her.

"I don't imagine he does, Mom," he teased gently. "Listen, I mean it. I would like your input about my plans and anyone else who would like to have a say, I'm willing to listen."

She shook her head. "You had to do that, didn't you?"

His brows lifted. "Do what?"

"Spoil things by bringing up the fact that you came here to change everything." She started the car. "Goodbye, Mr. McKenna."

She hoped that Rob was the type of guy who talked about doing something for a long time before he got around to acting on it.

She put the truck in gear and drove off. Soon she was in town and pulling into Pinetop Hardware. She grabbed the materials list from the seat and made her way to the door. As soon as she entered the store, the smell of Rob's cologne was replaced by the smell of paint and pesticides.

It wasn't long before the manager tailed her. Scott Carson was always a bit too friendly when she was in the store.

"Afternoon, Celia," he said. "Can I help you with something?"

"I have the materials list." She waved it above her head. "The things we'll need for the Christmas floats."

"Let me see." Scott was good looking and a nice man. It was a shame she didn't click with him. He'd probably make someone a nice boyfriend or even a husband. Sometimes Celia longed for one or the other, but she was glad she had neither. She came from the camp of once burned, always shy because twice shy wasn't enough.

"How about I price it out for you?" He walked toward his desk. "I'm working on a materials list for the Harvest Festival now. I guess they want to do an American Idol theme but Pinetop style."

Celia was not on the committee, so this was pleasant news to her. It sounded like fun to hear the townsfolk show off their talents. Last year they had a pie contest and Mary Whatley won with her triple berry, double-crusted number. Celia had entered her strawberry rhubarb and got an honor-able mention.

Funny how Rob asked what the town harvested. That was obvious. They harvested goodwill and the concept of community.

While Scott was pricing out her materials, she could head over to the thrift shop and make up for lost time.

"Thanks, Rob," she said with a smile.

"Come again?" he asked, his face tight with a frown.

She hadn't even known what made her say that name.

"Who's Rob?" he demanded more than asked.

"I apologize. I meant Scott," she said. "I don't know what I was thinking."

Yes, she did. She was thinking tall, tousled hair, and handsome. She popped a few quarters into the soda machine on her way out and bought herself a diet cola. After that Freudian slip, she needed a drink.

She waved to Scott and smiled again to make up for her misstep. Why was Rob McKenna in her every thought and on the tip of her tongue?

CHAPTER FOUR

ROB

The first ride in his new truck was into town with Lucky riding shotgun. He didn't need any permits for his fence, so ordering the supplies straight from the hardware store was the next thing on his list. On the phone, the manager assured him he could refer him to someone who could handle the whole thing.

Faded cursive letters hardly showed on the weathered hardware store sign. It took him back in time, as though years between his past and now had all but melted away. Though he was a native son, it had been a lifetime since he'd been back to Pinetop.

A gust of wind blew past him. With the weather being unpredictable and a cold front moving in, he found his crew neck sweater and the denim jacket he wore insufficient.

Lucky hopped out as soon as Rob opened his door. They walked together into the store. Not once did his new furry companion pull on the leather leash.

The building was deceiving. The inside was much larger than the outside suggested. Careful rows of lumber stretched from the concrete floors to high ceilings. Tidy shelves of everything from lawn tools to snow shovels lined the aisles of the rest of the store.

He stopped in the main aisle to read the signs directing him to fencing materials. He found what he was looking for and scoured the area for an employee. Coming up empty-handed, he walked to the service desk for help.

"Hi," he said to a burly man with shaggy brown hair.

"Howdy," the man answered.

Rob thought he recognized him.

"Scott? Scott Carson?"

"Yeah. Oh, my goodness, you're Bobby McKenna." He reached over the counter and pounded Rob on the shoulder.

"I go by Rob now." He realized he might have to do that a lot until people got to know him again.

Scott was one of the few football players who hadn't hazed him mercilessly in high school. In part because they were the same age and by the time Scott played football, Rob was big enough to defend himself.

"Rob." He said his name as if it solved a puzzle.

"Yeah," he said. "Kind of hard to have people take you seriously in business when you put Bobby on the contracts."

"I got you. My grandmother still calls me Scotty."

He looked over his shoulder toward the fencing supplies. "I put a new house on my property and need a fence for this guy." He ruffled the fur on Lucky's head.

"You're the one who called."

"Yes." He handed Scott the rough drawing with the measurements and told him the kind of fencing he wanted.

"We can get you set up. Once I see your permit, we can start. You can order the material, but it will sit around until the permits are in. With this weather, it's not a good idea to wait. Not the ideal time for fence building in the Rockies."

Scott had a pleasant enough demeanor, but Rob couldn't shake the feeling that there was some underlying tension between them.

"You're talking because I picked something out that's taller than four feet, right?" he asked.

"Exactly." Scott looked him directly in the eye. "You can do four feet without a problem."

"The guy in the permits department said go ahead, wink, wink." Rob laughed.

"I'm not that guy," Scott replied with a voice as cold as his eyes. "There's a big difference between what we want and what we can have."

Was he talking about something other than fencing?

Rob attempted to plead his case. "You know where I live, right? It's out in the middle of nowhere. The four-foot rule has to do with obstructing views. The guy gave me the go-ahead."

"I'm not that guy."

He felt himself tense and knew if he threw a big city fit, they would brand him as difficult. "Fine," he said, throwing up his hands in a truce. "You're right. I'll pick out something else. How about a pallet fence?"

"That we can do," he said. "We'll have to do it quickly. We're expecting the ground to freeze solid by the end of the month. I can come out and dig the fence posts say ... day after tomorrow." He looked at Rob's drawing and counted. "After that, I can do this in a day, two tops." He stared straight into his eyes. "Does that work for you?"

"That would be great." Rob's voice didn't show the frustration still plaguing his body.

"Outstanding," said Scott. "Say ..."

"Yeah?" asked Rob.

"You haven't by any chance run into Celia Roberts since you've been back, have you?"

"I have. We share a property line."

"Big Victorian on the other side?" asked Scott with a dark smile.

"That's it, but you can't really call us neighbors since my place is on the far end of my mom's land."

"Good." Scott dropped Rob's drawing onto the counter.

That was an odd response. "Why do you ask?"

"I just wouldn't want the fence building to bother her or her guests."

"Right." He started to walk away but Scott called him back.

"I'll going to tally this up, and I'll need a fifty percent down payment. I have a standard contract for this kind of project, but we can use the store's acceptance of your payment if that works."

If Rob couldn't have the fence he wanted because of rules, he wouldn't let Scott off that easily. He turned the tables.

"Well now," he said with a smile. "Since you're a by the book kind of guy, I wouldn't want you to lower your standards for me. You were right about the fence. I think we should be consistent, don't you? As soon as we have a materials list, then I'll sign the contract and give you a check. Sound good?"

Scott nodded. Something was up with him for sure. He wasn't unfriendly, but he wasn't nice either.

He thought it was too good to be true that Pinetop would have no memory of him being bullied for being a bastard. Reputations were hard to come by in the big city and hard to lose in small towns, but he wouldn't lose sleep over it.

He loaded Lucky into the truck and drove home.

As he pulled into the driveway, he saw Jackson's dented truck out front, waiting for him. It was one of his dog walking days and Rob had almost forgotten.

"Hey, sorry, man," he called out as Jackson exited the truck. "Kind of hard to walk the dog when I have the dog."

"No worries," said Jackson. "I brought my mom. She kept me company."

Rob hid his smile. Seeing Celia was like a lottery win.

She slid out from the passenger side and walked around to join her son.

"Celia, do you like tea?" Rob asked.

"Hmm." She shrugged like she could take it or leave it.

"Are you kidding?" asked Jackson. "She drinks it like she's from England."

"Does she?" Rob flashed a grin as he stared her down.

Rob set Lucky free. The dog was over the moon excited to see the boy, who came equipped with a ball. He removed the dog's leash and Lucky took off. When Jackson tossed the ball, both boy and dog disappeared around the back of the house.

Rob headed to Celia and said, "Why on earth would you say no when you mean yes?"

"I didn't come for tea."

"I don't imagine you did, but I have some excellent peach that I mix with milk to make peaches and cream. Then I have some hibiscus, which is my favorite. I also have—"

"I got the picture," she interrupted. "I'd love some tea."

"Good." He rubbed his arms. "It's cold out here. Let's go inside to get warm. I'll show you the house and the view. We'll have tea and sit by the fire until Jackson wears the dog out or the other way around."

"You're out here by yourself." She stepped onto the stone walkway that led to the front door.

"It's kind of nice. It's peaceful." He leaned forward, careful not to crowd her while he unlocked the door. "And here we are."

She stepped inside and halted. "It's lovely. Much nicer than I imagined."

"Not bad for a pretend Victorian," he ribbed.

"It isn't bad at all." She drifted forward, but he noticed she was taking it all in.

"Follow me." He led her to the back of the house which faced the wooded acres he owned. The wall of windows, which strayed from the Victorian design, looked out onto the wild land beyond.

"I hope you forgive the creative license to stray from classic design, but the land is beautiful to look at. I couldn't cover it up. Plus, this view will help me sell it to investors."

He regretted that comment instantly as he watched her shoulders stiffen and her expression sour.

He quickly changed the subject. "Look at that." He pointed to Jackson and the dog in total sync pitching and retrieving the ball.

"He loves that dog," she said with a note of sadness.

"I like him too, but if Jackson would rather keep him, I'd be happy to let him have him." He guided her into the kitchen where he filled a teapot with water and placed it on the stovetop.

"I can't have a dog in the inn."

He studied her.

"Lot of upkeep," he said sympathetically. "More work. I got you. Jackson's welcome to play here anytime with Lucky." He pointed to her son. "That right there is a thing of beauty."

"It's nice to see him happy."

"And Jackson too," joked Rob. "Lucky is nice and all, but I don't do for him what your son does." The teapot let out a whistle. "Let's have that tea."

He walked her to the table. "I met a friend of yours," he said. "Pinetop Hardware? The manager?"

"Scott?" she asked. "Sure. He's a friend. He's helping us with the materials for our festival and parade."

"Ah," he said. "He's helping me with a fence. I'll put up a small fence to keep Lucky in. Kind of weird to put something permanent around a house built to move. I wanted to make the fence higher, but looking out, I see that would have been foolish. The view is more incredible than I realized."

Her smile was tight. "Not for long."

He set out two cups. "Does Jackson like tea?" He thought about getting a third cup.

"Jackson is not a fan of tea or coffee. He tried his hand at drinking coffee once on an empty stomach and decided adult beverages weren't his thing," she said with a laugh.

"He's sixteen?"

"Yep. Hard to believe."

He did the math and his eyes grew wide. "You were preg-nant in—"

"High school," she finished. "I went half days during my senior year."

That bit of information shocked Rob. He tried not to show his surprise. The math had been at the back of his mind when he'd learned she was Jackson's mom.

"I'll say it again. He's a nice kid. You've done a great job." He set out a box of mixed tea bags and handed her a cup of hot water.

She chose the peach and dunked her tea bag aggressively.

Jackson burst through the front door with Lucky panting hard right behind him.

"Would you like to join us for tea?" Rob hoped he'd say yes, so they would stay longer. He was afraid he had brought up a subject that caused her pain and judging by the look on her face, he had.

"No, but thanks." The boy brushed the air with his hand. "Not much of a tea drinker."

"I have soda." Rob went to the refrigerator and pulled out a six-pack of root beer. "My friend made these." He uncapped a bottle and handed it over.

"Looks like a real beer." Jackson grinned as he took a sip.

"Hey," scolded Celia. "No beer for you."

"Just joking, Mom."

Rob reached to the top of the fridge to get Lucky a treat.

"There," he said. "Now we're all good."

Celia took a couple polite sips, but it was clear she was ready to leave. A thick gust of wind swept against the house, carrying with it thick clouds. Jackson moved to the glass to watch the storm move in.

"Oh," he said excitedly. "Snow. I can totally feel it in the air."

That was one thing a Coloradan knew, thought Rob—when it would snow. His mother always got a headache the day before a storm. The older folks complained about their bones creaking, but somehow everyone always knew when bad weather was on its way.

"Don't say that." Celia groaned. "Not yet anyway. I'm not ready for the winter."

"Were they calling for snow?" Rob pulled his tea bag from his cup and added cream and sugar. "Seems out of the blue."

"This is an unexpected storm." Her tone contained a hint of dread. "Albuquerque low which means lots of wet snow."

"Cheer up. This is good. This is what we need. A few customers who come and get snowbound," Jackson said with a laugh.

"Yeah, but then I'd have to feed them without notice. They would complain it wasn't their fault it snowed."

"It's not yours either, Mom. You think everything is your fault, and it's not," Jackson said.

Out of the mouths of babes, thought Rob.

"Thanks for outing me." She rolled her eyes at her son.

"I'll be right back." Rob dashed to his desk and wrote Jackson a check.

"Here you go," he said. "This is for today. I'm putting up a fence if you want to lend a hand with that and earn some extra cash. I don't know if you're handy or not, but the offer is there if your mother says it's okay." The kid needed a truck repair and his mother was not the type to accept hand-outs, so Rob figured good honest work would do the trick.

"I don't know how to work with tools," Jackson admitted.

"Here's your chance to learn." He stared out the window "Open invitation. I invited your mother to look over the plans I have for the land outside. I'm putting in a resort. There will be lots of opportunities heading your way."

"Cool," said Jackson. "Yeah, maybe."

Rob could tell he was ready to leave. "I'll walk you two out. Take the bottle with you if you haven't finished."

Jackson walked ahead.

Celia grabbed Rob's arm firmly.

He looked to her hand clutching his forearm and then glanced at her.

"Why did you do that?" she asked.

"What?" He was genuinely at a loss.

"You told him about the development."

"I'm not sure what the problem is," he said.

"You'll never get it."

"What is it, exactly?" He'd been sympathetic to her, but he would not let her off the hook.

"Never mind," she said.

"No," he insisted, but Jackson stepped back into the house.

"Mom, are you coming?"

"Yep, I'll be right there." She stopped and looked at him. "Thanks for the tea." She dashed off toward her son.

Rob didn't understand Celia at all. Didn't understand how he could remember the girl who did nothing to help him back then and yet wanted to help her now. What was it about her that pulled at his heart?

CHAPTER FIVE

CELIA

On the ride home, the first snowflake hit the windshield. Celia sat wondering why it was him that twisted her up so much. She hadn't felt this upset since those days after her ex-husband had walked out the door and disappeared.

"Are you okay with coming over and taking care of the dog?" she asked Jackson.

"Yeah, Lucky's great."

"And you don't think it's a little over the top for him to pay you so much for each visit?"

He gave her a quick glance before his eyes went back to the road. "What's your point?"

Her son was direct. Even if he weren't a teenager, Celia was sure he'd have no filter. She would never say so, but his father had been that way, and it often worried her that nature would overrule nurture. She wasn't the kind of parent to punish her son for his father's sins.

"Just wondered if he heard something ... I don't know ... like we're charity." She looked out the window at the blanket of snow falling from the sky.

"You think he feels sorry for us? Maybe someone told him about Dad?" He turned on to their street.

"I'm not sure," she said. "I mean, he knew that I owned the inn before he stopped by to let me know he would ruin all that land of his."

"Developing it doesn't mean he's ruining it, Mom. It means he's using it." Jackson lifted his shoulders. "I like the idea of learning how to use tools. I thought I lost the chance to do that when Dad left."

Celia knew the day would come when Jackson would feel the emptiness from not having a father figure. When he'd gotten the job at Pinetop Grocer, it thrilled her. There were so many square peg men there that would be a good influence on him. She would never get remarried just to give Jackson a new dad, but their conversation made her look inward to her needs and his.

It had been many years. Celia's way of dealing with the pain was to seal herself off and put on a happy if not dutiful front. She sank herself into her business because while stressful and risky, a canceled reservation might break the bank, but it would not break her heart.

Here this stranger, though he was a hometown boy returned, threatened her carefully laid out life with his random kindness.

"Okay," she said. "I'm just trying to teach you to look before you leap."

"I'm not leaping," he said. "I'm trying new things. You see change as the end of things. I see it as the beginning."

He was never disrespectful to her, though his frankness sometimes caught her off guard. Often, he was right. She had taken for granted that he needed her constant counsel, when in fact, he had some valuable perspective of his own to offer.

He parked the truck, and they headed inside.

Celia thought about the dog and looked around the inn and wondered why they couldn't have Lucky if Rob thought it was better for him and Jackson. She'd said no but not because of the work. Jackson would take care of him. It was because she didn't want to lose control with something even mildly unpredictable as the day-to-day life with a dog.

"Hey, bud," she called up the stairs to him.

Jackson was halfway to his room at the top of the house, a dormer room which, despite his age, he kept neat.

"Yeah?" He leaned over the rail to look down at her.

"What if we took Lucky?"

Her son's posture straightened, and his lips spread into a smile that nearly split his beautiful face.

"Really?"

"Yeah. I like him. You like him. We have a fence. He isn't a hummingbird, but the Hummingbird Inn could use a mascot."

"We could strap wings to his back," Jackson said. "He wouldn't mind."

And for the first time since she could remember, he bounded toward her, taking the steps two at a time, and gave her a big hug.

"Okay," she giggled. "I think I have Rob's number around here somewhere. He left it on the phone table. Go look."

She followed him into the parlor. Rectangular windows that let the outside light in bordered the front door. It was snowing heavily and accumulating quickly. If she had any chance of getting the dog over here, she needed to act fast.

"Do you want to call him or should I?" she asked. "I mean, you know him better than I do."

"Whatever." He lifted his shoulders into a shrug. "I think since you said yes, you should call him."

She tried not to seem too eager to call Rob, but it felt a little like she had a life outside the Hummingbird Inn making the call. Her mouth felt dry, and a lump stuck in her throat. Outside her earlier call to him to complain, she hadn't called a man in a lifetime, and it was scary.

"Do you think he was serious about giving us the dog? You don't think he said it just to say it, right?" She held the phone in her hand.

"It's not the thing you say to people, Mom. Be real."

"Okay," she said, finding her nerve. She dialed his number. He took a moment to answer.

"Rob McKenna."

"Hello, Mr. McKenna?" she said as he picked up. "This is Ms. Roberts, Jackson's mom."

When she glanced at Jackson, he rolled his eyes.

She turned her shoulder to him.

"Celia, good to hear from you. Everything okay?"

She loved the way his voice sounded happy. "Jackson and I were talking it over, and if you're serious about letting him have the dog, we would like to take you up on that offer."

"Oh, wow," he said. "Yeah, okay. That would save me the hassle of building a fence. I think Lucky kind of belongs to Jackson, anyway. All you have to do is see them together to know that."

"Yes, I agree." Emotion warbled her words, but the tension released from her spine. Her voice changed from emotional to happy while she talked to him.

"I know it's coming down hard, but I could give my new truck a test drive and bring Lucky over."

"Are you sure?" She mouthed the word *now* to Jackson, who nodded enthusiastically. She hated to see Rob come out in the storm only to deliver the dog. "I'm about to make dinner. Why don't you plan to stay if you have nothing else to do? I was going to do a spin on barbecue pork."

Jackson's jaw dropped, and that made her smile. They didn't invite anyone to the house for dinner unless they were paying guests, and it felt so good she had to stifle her laugh.

"Okay," he said. "See you in a few minutes."

As soon as she was off the phone, Jackson launched into a full-blown mimicry of the conversation.

"Oh, Rob." He placed his hand over his heart and gave her an over-the-top swoon.

"You better stop, young man." She reached over and goosed him at the waist where he was ticklish.

"Oh, I agree, Rob," he continued, as he dodged her.

She looked down at the phone and to her horror it wasn't all the way hung up. She nudged it into place and waltzed into her kitchen in an extraordinarily good mood.

"Shall we have pork for dinner tonight?" she asked Jackson. "I can glaze it with that Chinese sauce you like so much."

"Sounds great." He leaned on the counter. "So he's coming?"

Celia smiled from ear to ear, happy to confirm the good news.

"Yes, he's putting Lucky in his truck now. Now wash up and set the table because we have a dinner guest."

CHAPTER SIX

ROB

It was coming down steadily as Rob loaded Lucky into the truck. It had been ages since he'd driven in the snow but having a heavy all-wheel-drive truck would make it easier.

What had been longer was going over to someone's house for a nice meal. But at the rate the snow was falling, maybe he would have to take a raincheck—more like a snow check. If he stayed at the Hummingbird Inn for any length of time on a night like this, he would have to check in as a guest.

The cloud cover made the night look more progressed than it was. Rob's lights were brilliant lanterns cutting through the heavy snowfall as he parked in front of the inn.

"Come on, Lucky."

It tugged at his heart that he was parting with the dog. For a moment, he thought he had acted too hastily. He'd never given himself the chance to settle down or become attached to much of anything. He'd learned that lesson from his mother. She'd raised him like he was a business deal. His father, like Jackson's, had taken off and left his mother on her own. The only good thing was that Fiona McKenna had the money in his family. His father was a handsome face that attracted her. When it came time to settle down, his father had no interest in being part of a family.

Was that how it had been with Celia and Jackson Sr.? It seemed odd that Jackson had taken his mother's last name just as he had. Maybe his draw to the boy and Celia was one of commiseration.

Having no way to model what a good relationship should be, he was all business. The next deal had always been his mistress. Only now, it felt natural driving along with the dog as his partner, and he wondered if he'd missed out on both life and love.

Rob climbed down from the truck and helped the dog out. As soon as Lucky hit the ground, he bounded across the yard, frolicking in the powdery snow that had covered the grass. He moved in circles, barking at Rob as though he were trying to get him to play.

Jackson opened the door of the inn with gusto. "C'mon Lucky," he called, patting his thighs. Without hesitation, the beast scampered inside.

Celia appeared at the doorway. She was a petite woman, but next to her tall son, she looked like a small child. He ambled up the short walk, grinning with satisfaction that he'd made the right choice.

"Well, that went well." The dog was thrilled with Jackson, and if Celia's smile was any sign, she was happy with him.

"Thanks for that." She leaned in as if she might hug him and thought better of it. "I can't tell you how much this means to him."

"I think I know." Rob didn't know Jackson, but he had his guesses. Rob had been a lonely kid for most of his growing-up years. In a way, the bullying had forged his sense of autonomy. It helped him stay focused on his goals. However, there were days and nights as a young boy when he could have used a companion like Lucky. Back then his mother didn't allow animals in the house.

Celia closed the door behind them. As he kicked off the snow from his boots, he noticed the mess he'd made. He looked around to figure out the way to the kitchen for something to wipe up the snow.

"What are you looking for?" she asked.

"A towel?"

"I'll get one. Take your shoes off and get comfortable."

He talked louder so she could hear. "It's coming down hard. I'll unload Lucky's food and stuff for Jackson, and then I should hit the road."

"Oh." She returned with the towel.

Was that disappointment he saw in her expression?

"Unless"—his eyes focused on her pouting lips—"dinner is already on."

"Well, yeah," she said.

"I didn't mean to be rude," he whispered. "I was only thinking of your convenience."

"It's no bother," she said. "We'll figure it out. You probably haven't had a decent meal since you got here."

He laughed. "I haven't had one in ages. For the last few years, I can safely say everything has been indecent."

Rob knew as soon as his words were out, they came out wrong. "I don't even know what that meant."

"It's okay," she said. "You're a bachelor. I think indecent is a requirement."

"That's not what I meant." He wondered if she pictured him eating sushi off a naked woman's body. "I just said something dumb trying to make a play on words, and it didn't work. I wasn't referring to my love life. Because my love life is nothing but business deals."

She rolled her eyes like she didn't believe him.

"What?"

"Nothing," she whispered. "I'll start dinner."

"If you haven't started, can I help?"

"Can you cook?" she asked.

"I have a few tricks up my sleeve." He wiped up the melted snow with the towel. "Eating out got old quickly. I learned to whip up a few things I could enjoy." He followed her into the kitchen where she took the towel and tossed it into a basket set in the corner. "What's on deck?"

"Well," she said, eyeballing the cupboard, "I planned to make a pork roast but that might take too long."

He looked over her shoulder at the ingredients she had on hand.

"How about pizza?" he asked.

"Pizza?"

He reached over her for a bag of flour and packets of yeast.

"This will be quick and it's in my lane. Do you mind if I take over your kitchen and make something for you?"

"Well—"

"Right, you were going to make barbecue and here I am taking over."

"No, it's okay." She moved back and took a seat at the table.

"Are you sure? If your heart is set on pork, I don't want to change your mind."

She looked lost, like she didn't know how to answer an offer of someone taking care of her for a change. There was a pause between them, and it gave Rob an opportunity to study her. Neither of them was old by any means. She was by his calculations thirty-three and he'd just turned thirty-four.

She was so pretty. The same perfect hair from high school fell past her shoulders in a quieter, simpler style. Not as fussy as it had been when they were in the tenth grade. He would have sworn she'd spent hours on it then, highlighting it, blowing it dry, curling it, but now it looked effortless.

Rob opened a cabinet door, guessing where the stemware might be. He took down two wine glasses and found a bottle of chardonnay in the fridge. He drew the bottle out and poured her a glass.

"You relax and keep me company while I make you dinner. How does that sound?"

She lifted the glass. "Aren't you going to join me?"

"Sure." He splashed the glass with a taste and held it out to hers for a toast.

"Cheers." Next, he made sure the oven was empty, and he turned the knob to preheat. Pizza was his specialty. He mixed the dry yeast with warm water into an empty bowl he found in the middle of the table.

"Usually it has fruit in it," she said.

"Good thing it's empty today."

He could feel her watch his every move. Was it because she didn't trust his skills, or was it because no one ever cooked for her? He imagined it was the latter because there was no concern in her eyes when he glanced at her.

When the yeast foamed to his satisfaction, he shook some flour into the bowl. He salted and stirred it until it came together, then kneaded it a few times and let it rest.

"Wow."

"Yeah," he said. "I figure if I was going to ruin myself on pizza, I might as well make it. The process is very therapeutic."

"I serve flatbreads to the guests, but I get the pre-made crusts from Jackson's store."

"Oh, is it Jackson's store?" he teased.

"Yeah," she smiled. "That's how I think of it, anyway."

"You'll have to make me something off your menu some time."

"That was the idea, before you took over my kitchen."

"I thought you might like a break." He kneaded the dough a few more times. "But if you mind, I'm happy to turn it over to you."

"No, have at it." She waved him off. "I'm learning something watching you."

He hoped it was that all men weren't awful.

He wiped a baking sheet with a paper towel dabbed in oil. He floured the dough, rolled it out quickly, and laid it on the sheet.

"Okay, now comes the good stuff." He pointed to the refrigerator. "Mind if I get in your goodies?"

Without missing a beat, Celia quipped, "Why, I thought you'd never ask."

Rob fired her a look. He couldn't hide his attraction and feeling the spark between them warmed him.

His attention turned to her fridge where he found what he needed. He mixed up a personal recipe for pizza sauce and topped the crust with a mishmash of various cheeses and herbs.

"Now," he said. "This is where you come in. Help me decide what should go on this."

"Jackson likes meat. Hamburger, sausage, pepperoni," she answered.

"And what does Celia like?" he whispered. "I'm sure Jackson could eat a whole pizza, but why don't each of us take a third? What do you want on your third?"

"I like feta cheese and veggies." She came to life and ducked under his arm that was holding open the door of the refrigerator. She stepped in front of him so she could gather what she wanted.

"And what do you like?" she asked as she bent over.

Celia's amazing backside butted against his thighs. Her question instantly became a loaded one.

"Oops," she said. "Pardon me."

Rob wanted to reply, "No, forgive me" because her clumsiness sent sexy thoughts racing through his mind. She was firm and obviously made time for the gym, though he was sure Pinetop didn't have one so that meant running the inn was a workout for her.

"I'll have whatever you're having. I've done my part," he said. "You do the toppings."

"I like the top," she said with the first authentic smile he'd seen since they got acquainted.

Their bodies were close as they danced around each other, smiling at the risk of accidentally colliding. Rob looked out the window to check on the snow.

"Wow, that was so fast."

"Piling up?" she asked.

He watched her use cooking shears instead of a knife to julienne the peppers. She set it aside and broke out an egg pan.

"I like to brown the sausage. I'll throw together a salad to go with the pizza, so my teenage termite is fully fed," she teased.

"Eats a lot, does he?"

"Don't you remember when you were his age?"

"I do." His mother used to tell him he could eat through a week's worth of groceries in a day.

"I feel like I've lived the last sixteen years in this kitchen," she joked.

"All by yourself?" he asked.

There was a quick shift in the atmosphere. It was like a storm-cloud hovered above them, and Rob regretted the question. It was way too soon and bad timing during their nice moment to bring up what felt like it might be a sad subject.

"Mostly," she answered.

Against his better judgment, Rob continued. "So … Jackson —big Jackson was two years ahead of you and me—"

"Yep, I was seventeen, and he was nineteen. It wasn't easy," she answered.

"You've done a fine job." He tried to lighten the moment with a well-deserved compliment. "On both your son and the pizza. Let's put that sausage on and put this beauty into the oven."

She turned off the flame and went through the motions of topping the rest of the pizza. The light mood of earlier disappeared.

"I hope I didn't say the wrong thing."

She shook her head. "It's not you. I've never been sure why people get so darn curious about a young mother. Things happen. Bad decisions can be blessings in disguise."

"I'm not sure why either," he said.

She put the pan in the oven and swirled around to retrieve her glass. She tipped the bottle into it, filling it to the top, and lifted it to her lips to drink. It was a medicinal sip.

He wished he could go back in time and make the conversation go a different way.

Celia leaned over and hit an intercom switch and called for Jackson. In minutes, he and Lucky bolted through a side door.

"What smells so good?" he asked.

"Dinner." She didn't sound short or angry, but she wasn't the same perky person who had been glad to see him earlier.

"Can Lucky lay under the table?" Jackson asked.

"We can try it, but if he bothers us, he has to be put away." She looked at him and the dog and smiled. "Dinner should be ready in another ten minutes. Wash up."

"I got it," he said happily, and dashed off to wash his hands. Lucky moved after him like a shadow.

Celia's eyes cut to Rob as if to say *don't ask about his father in front of him.*

"Don't worry," he said. "I learned my lesson."

CHAPTER SEVEN

CELIA

Jackson set the big table they reserved for guests with cloth napkins and fancy cutlery.

Rob lit the candles. When the food was served, even though it was only pizza, everything was beautiful.

Celia felt bad she had gotten riled earlier. Now she was trying to calm down. She would be a fool to waste what could be a nice moment for all of them.

Rob pulled out her chair like a gentleman and acted like she hadn't been rude to him. Maybe he was being polite and waiting till dinner was over to never speak to her again.

She sat next to Jackson. After he cut the pizza, Rob sat across from them both.

"You guys made this?" asked Jackson, whose voice still squeaked with puberty.

"Got to put a little oil on that voice, bud," Rob ribbed with a warm smile.

With his teasing, the tension in her evaporated.

Jackson laughed hard enough to double him over.

"My mom calls me bud too." He broke off a piece of pizza to give to the dog, but Rob stopped him.

"Not a good idea." Authority rang out in his voice, but he wasn't unkind. "That could kill him. It has onions. They're not good for dogs. Neither are grapes nor chocolate."

"Oh." Jackson set the bite on the edge of his plate. "I didn't know."

"I looked stuff up as soon as he wound up on my doorstep." Rob's tone softened. "The rule seems to be, don't feed him your food, and he won't feed you his."

Jackson laughed again. They were on a roll.

"So will the snow kill your business this weekend?" Rob asked.

"No." She nursed the wine they'd poured in the kitchen. "It shouldn't. We'll have the roads plowed. I have a guy at Pinetop Hardware who always gets me cleared out."

"Would that be Scott?"

She knitted her brows. "That's the second time you've mentioned him."

"He didn't seem to like the fact that I knew you." Rob sipped his wine.

"Scott's over the top but very helpful when I'm in the store."

"Very helpful." Jackson finger-quoted the words.

"That seems to be the truth." She remembered calling Scott 'Rob' and how he hadn't liked that. She would have told him the story except she didn't want to admit he was on her mind when she made the mistake.

"Helpful nice or helpful creepy?" asked Rob.

"He might have a thing for me." She could feel her cheeks warm. Was it the wine or Rob?

Jackson snickered at her choice of words.

"Jackson," she warned.

Rob joined her son in laughter and soon the table was infected.

"Scott has a thing ..." mocked Jackson.

"Okay, that's enough." Celia put her hand up before he crossed a line.

"The second she's in the store, he's tailing her, asking her if he can help her. He's on her like lint on tape."

"That's funny." Rob lifted his glass to his lips and finished his splash of wine. "No one was eager to help me. I had to track him down. It was weird too because he gave me a tough time about building my fence. I'll take great delight in canceling that order."

"Aw ... you aren't building a fence for Lucky which means I won't learn how to use any tools." Jackson's tall frame slumped in his seat.

"I don't expect I need one. What do you think?" Rob asked.

"I was looking forward to learning construction."

"There will be no shortage of my need for help. The resort will provide many opportunities to work. If you help, then you'll bring Lucky, won't you?" He rubbed the scruff on his chin. "I might have to think this through. A fence might be a wise investment after all."

"Let's not spoil dinner with talk of deforestation and destruction."

She made her request with as endearing a smile as she could muster.

Rob looked at her, his eyes twinkling with warmth and allure.

"We have to talk about it sometime."

"Not now please," she requested again. "I'm liking you right this minute."

He held up his hands in a sign of truce. "Okay, I'd hate to ruin my good luck."

"And you don't have to build a fence for the dog," she said, shaking her head.

"I'll still think about it."

She caught herself smiling at him.

He too lingered, tilting his head with the same winsome expression.

She took a deep breath. Jackson looking on made her feel self-conscious. She straightened and reached for his empty plate. They'd made a good dent in dinner. It was time for something sweeter. She had a frozen yogurt cake she could top with a raspberry sauce in a matter of a few minutes.

"Do you two fellas have room for dessert and coffee?"

"What do we have?" asked Jackson.

"Yogurt cake."

"Can I have mine with chocolate syrup and a glass of milk?"

"Yep. What you about, Rob?" She turned to him and lifted a brow. "Anything I could interest you in?"

He gave her a look that said he'd like a lot more than cake and coffee. How long had it been since a man looked at her like that? Scott from the hardware store didn't count because she had no interest in him, but Rob was a different story. Did she want to offer him more?

"Coffee and cake sound wonderful, but I should hit the road. Let me check on that snow."

"Stay here," Jackson blurted. "I mean, if it's too deep, stay the night."

Celia knew her son didn't understand the looks that were being passed between the two of them. All he considered was they had enough rooms in the inn for him to stay if he needed to. They rose from the table with plates in hand, taking them back into the kitchen.

Celia commandeered them, sliding the scraps into the trash and rinsing the plates off while Jackson took the cake out of the freezer.

"What can I do?" Rob asked.

Celia looked over her shoulder as she loaded the dishwasher. She glanced at the two men and saw the actions of a family. Her late ex-husband never pitched in for meals, cleaned up, or ate with them. He devoured his food as fast as he could and left the table. That was if he came home. He spent most of Jackson's younger years missing in action. He'd leave for months at a time without a word.

Rob was a natural at the whole domestic thing. He and Jackson side by side looked right. She shook her head. She couldn't let herself romanticize the moment, though it made her wonder if she was ready for something more.

"How are you at making coffee?"

"I'm an excellent barista." Rob moved in closer to her.

Jackson chuckled. "Can we keep him, Mom?"

Celia wasn't sure if it pleased her that her son liked Rob so much. Was having him around only setting them up for disappointment?

"Let's see if he's house-trained."

"Mom has jokes." Jackson needed no direction as he set the table again, only this time for the yogurt cake. It was plain vanilla and since Jackson suggested the chocolate sauce, she didn't bother with her raspberry one.

The pungent fragrance of coffee cut through the air. Rob made the coffee good and strong which would be great, except it meant she wouldn't sleep well that night, and Celia loved her sleep. She peeked through the kitchen window to check the snow and feared that Rob might, in fact, be snowbound.

"Guys," she said.

They closed in around her as she looked out the window. Rob and Jackson were a good six inches taller.

"Wow," remarked Jackson and then he clutched Rob's shoulder. "Looks like you're spending the night for sure."

Rob and Celia glanced at one another. The coffee pot sputtered, signaling it was just about finished.

"Coffee's ready," Celia announced, changing the subject.

"I'll take Lucky out," Jackson said. "I'll be right back." He left Celia and Rob alone.

She went through the motions of gathering cups for coffee. The attraction she felt for him was clear and no longer an underlying element or notion. It was like another presence floating in the room. She could feel him behind her on the verge of asking a question. She waltzed past him to the dining room table.

"Can you grab the coffee?" she asked. "Help yourself to the milk, or creamer, and sugar if that's how you like it."

"Hey," he said as he followed behind her.

She ignored him.

"Hey," he repeated.

He set the coffeepot on a trivet and took hold of her arm. They were so close she could feel the tickle of his arm hair. Her body reacted immediately. Racing heart. Sweaty palms. Pulsing in places that hadn't been touched in a decade. It was more than the fact that it had been a long time for her. There was a heady physical chemistry bouncing between them.

"I think I will have to spend the night here," he said with an arched brow.

"It's okay. It is an inn. I know you didn't expect to get trapped here."

"Trapped is not what I'm feeling." His fingers danced across her arm. "Are you okay with this?"

"Sure." She pulled her lower lip between her teeth. "And by tomorrow, if the snow lets up, they'll plow the drive between your place and mine."

He dropped his hand from her arm. Every cell missed his touch.

"I just wanted to make sure it was okay."

"It's fine," she repeated.

Jackson emerged through the front door with the dog, who galloped through the house, no doubt glad to be out of the cold snow.

Celia was grateful for the interruption of the moment between her and Rob. She wasn't used to any pounding of the heart, heating of the skin, twisting of her core moments.

"It's coming down, and it's deep." Jackson brushed a few flakes from his shoulders. "You may be here for a week."

Rob's eyes widened. "Seriously?"

"Just kidding, but you're here for the night for sure."

"It would seem," he said.

"Sweet! We can watch a movie." Jackson danced across the hardwood floor. "Or wait, do you play video games?"

Rob grinned. "I do not. Can you teach me?"

"I have two controllers," he said. "And my room is huge. I have two double beds."

Celia laughed. "He might want his own room. We can let him have a guest room." It occurred to her that no matter how big her son got she would always see the little boy in him.

The three of them sat at the table again as Celia served small wedges of frozen yogurt cake. Jackson was at the ready with the chocolate.

Rob had grown quiet.

"Everything okay?" she asked.

He lifted his eyes to her and replied with a deep, smoky gaze.

"I'm good." But the look he gave Celia was anything but good. She found it as delicious and decadent as the chocolate on the cake. No, not good, but something just north of wicked.

Jackson gobbled his dessert and hurried to his room. She knew he was setting things up so he and Rob could play a game.

"That's sweet of you to hang out with him. He only lets me have the other controller once in a while."

"I'm sure I'll enjoy it."

She had the urge to apologize for snapping when he'd asked about Jackson's birth.

"About earlier," she said.

"Yes."

"I didn't mean to be sensitive about the end of high school. Times are different, and I'm a grown woman. I took a lot of crap after graduation, and I'm weary of judgment."

"Understood. You're preaching to the choir here." He pointed to himself. "Bastard child."

"They were awful to you. Funny how Jackson goaded you, and yet he abandoned his son."

"What happened with you two?"

She sighed like the air leaked from her. "Life happened. He was a bully. I never stood up to him in anything." Celia remembered her ex was brutal to the younger male students, including Rob. "I'm sorry I never stuck up for you or the others."

"In hindsight, what could you have done? I don't understand the attraction. He wasn't nice."

She closed her eyes, trying to grab a snapshot of her younger self. "He was cute and popular. I was a teenage girl flattered by his attention." She gathered their dessert plates and stacked them on top of each other. "You're right about one thing, he wasn't a good guy," she said. "He didn't want to be a husband or a father, and I don't blame him. He was still a kid."

She didn't mean to tense, but a wave of emotion crested, and she felt paralyzed from the memories. Sometimes she could talk about it, and sometimes she couldn't.

"So were you." He finished his coffee and set the cup on the table with a thunk.

"I wouldn't miss having my son for anything in the world."

"Jackson's great, but it had to be hard," he said.

"It was hard and hurtful and not romantic. Jackson had a lot of problems and being a young man with a family didn't help much."

"So you divorced." It wasn't a question but a statement of fact as if he already had the details. Then again, it was a small town and people talked.

"Yeah, when Jackson was six," she said. "He went his way and never looked back. It wasn't much of a change because he wasn't around much anyway. I was always a single parent. When Jackson turned ten, he wanted to change his last name to Roberts. Since his father had signed all parental rights away, it was easy."

"You've done a remarkable job with everything, including this place." He looked up as if snatching a memory from above. "When I was a paperboy, I remember this house in high school. Mr. and Mrs. Campanella owned it. They were old and didn't have the money for repairs."

"Yep," she said. "It was old and beat up. When Jackson's dad left the first time, right before his birth, his parents helped me with the purchase. I told them what I wanted to do, and they felt bad for me and helped get the place."

"What a worthy investment."

Whether it was the emotional story, or the sugar, wine, carbs, and caffeine, vulnerability filled her. It would be easy to move closer and ask him for a hug.

Jackson appeared in the nick of time with Lucky at his heels.

"Ready." He bounced on the balls of his feet. Maybe cake and games were too much for him.

Rob rose. It felt like it would have been the most natural thing in the world for him to lean over and kiss her before he went to play a game with her son. As he passed her, Celia gazed upward to the ceiling, her face tilted like she was waiting for it.

CHAPTER EIGHT

ROB

Rob lifted his head from the pillow. He'd slept for a couple of hours, and then he woke up and couldn't fall back to sleep. He stared at the ceiling and counted the hummingbirds on the border while he waited for a reasonable hour to head downstairs.

When the sun peeked through a break in the curtains, he left his room and walked through the breezeway into the main house. He padded barefoot down the stairs to the kitchen, where he started coffee.

He had to give Celia credit. The inn was comfortable and provided all the amenities a person could want or need. Decorated tastefully, it preserved the Victorian charm without overdoing it.

Lucky quietly trotted into the kitchen and sat beside him. The sight of the dog gripped his heart. Being a dog owner wasn't in the cards for him, but it surprised him how much he liked the beast.

When the pot sputtered its final ounce, he poured himself a cup and stepped into the parlor and Lucky disappeared. Every so often he landed on a personal touch. There was a family picture of Celia and Jackson when he was young. Behind them stood Jackson Sr. It was a nice picture, but it seemed staged. Big Jackson's gaze was off to the sidelines, like he was forced to stay but his head was already somewhere else. He couldn't even fake a happy family life for a photo.

Rob picked up the picture so he could study every nuance of Celia, her sweet smile and her expressive eyes. Little Jackson was a cute kid too. His father wasn't present. He tried not to be hard on the man and attempted to put himself in Jackson Sr.'s shoes. The pressures of being a young dad had to be overwhelming, but he came to one conclusion. He wouldn't have left Celia or his son for anything. There wasn't anything he wouldn't have done to make it work for all of them. He believed that with everything he had, but then again, he had never really been in a longstanding relationship so how could he judge?

He peeked out the window to see the snow. The storm had been unexpected, and the volume of snowfall was off the charts.

The sky was blue, and the sun peeked above the horizon. He was ready to be home, a place only a little more familiar to him than Celia's inn, but he was eager to get away. Not away from Celia and Jackson, but away from the feelings that stirred within him when he was with them. Feelings that went against his core belief that he was an island—a man who needed nothing but his passion for business. The longer he stayed, the harder it got to lie to himself.

Out of nowhere, a big plow whooshed by and then a smaller Bobcat puttered along to Celia's driveway. A man hopped out wearing boots that came to his knees and removed the snow from her walkway.

Behind him, Celia danced across the wooden floor like she was checking to see if Santa had arrived. Her hair was drawn into a messy bun, with the fringe of her bangs framing her face. She was like a radiant sun bursting on to the scene.

"Wow," he said. "What's up?"

"Checking out the weather situation so I can confirm my guests." She stood next to him to look outside. "I can't afford to miss a weekend."

A weekend of cancellations to her would be like a big business deal falling through for him. Maybe worse since he imagined she didn't have a lot of money tucked away for leaner times.

He tugged on his shoes, which lay by the door. "I'll chase the street crew down to see if they'll clear mine next."

"They take care of them in order," she said. "I think I'm his last."

"I'll be your first," Rob teased. He thought about what it would be like to be the first man she could trust.

"What?" She turned and looked at him.

"Coffee is ready. I need to be out the door soon. I have a web conference with investors, and my equipment is at the house," he said. "We have to get the resort rolling."

She let out a sigh that turned into a growl. "You have a perfectly good house in your mother's home. You put together a silly prefab home, and now with the snow, you can't build until the spring. What's the rush?" she snapped.

"Touchy this morning. Is there something behind your harsh words?"

"I'm not sure," she said, hurrying to the kitchen. She helped herself to coffee as Rob joined her. He looked around for Lucky, who was nowhere in sight.

"Didn't you sleep well?"

She sipped her coffee and avoided his question.

"Coffee's fantastic."

"I'm glad you like it."

The snow removal equipment grew louder as though it were approaching the house, then it idled. There was a knock on the door. Celia rolled her eyes and set her cup on the counter.

She grumbled, "Scott."

Rob wondered if it was Scott who caused her bad mood or him. When she opened the front door, the golden Colorado sunlight bounced off the snow and lit up the entry.

"Hi," she said, her voice strained.

"Morning, Celia," he said. "Will your guests need to be leaving soon? We can dig them out."

"Guests?" she asked.

"The new truck out there." He leaned in and drew a deep breath. "Is that coffee I smell?" Without an invitation, he took a step forward.

Celia backed away from the door, letting him in.

He halted when his eyes fell on Rob, who stood in the doorway to the kitchen.

"Good morning." Rob didn't want to make trouble for Celia, but he savored the look of jealousy on Scott's face. "I'm the guest." He pointed to himself with a smile. "Shall I move my truck?"

"You'd be more useful if you got out and shoveled," Scott snapped.

Rob walked forward to look out the front window.

"You've created a wall of snow behind me. You expect me to shovel it?"

"I suppose we can dig you out if it will help you get on your way." If dirty looks were daggers, Rob would hemorrhage by the number thrown at him.

"I appreciate it. I'll be out of here as soon as you do."

He thought that might create an incentive for Scott, who was not pleased to see him.

"Did you want coffee, Scott?" Celia asked with pressed politeness.

"No, that's fine." He shook his head. "I'll dig this guy out and be moving on."

"Say, Scott," asked Rob. "How does the road look from here to my place?"

"You can follow us if you like. We'll head out that way and circle back around."

"Don't wait for me." Rob walked to the door and waited for Scott to step over the threshold. "I'll be out after Celia and I enjoy a coffee together."

He closed the door, locking Scott out.

"Come." He laid his arm over her shoulders and led her into the kitchen. "Let's have our coffee. Would you like a little toast or something to go with it?"

Just as they sat at the kitchen table, a ruckus that sounded like thunder tore down the stairs and Lucky and his boy appeared. Jackson bundled up to go outdoors.

"No school!" he bellowed.

"How is it on days you don't have to go to school you're up at the break of daylight, but on days you do, I can't pry you from under the covers?" Celia asked.

"Murphy's Law, Mom. Murphy's Law."

"Isn't that anything that can go wrong will?" she asked.

"That too." He opened the fridge and chugged from a bottle of milk.

"Jackson Matthew," she scolded.

"Gotta take the dog out, sorry, Mom." He was out the door with Lucky in seconds flat.

Celia turned to Rob. "That dog is magic." She craned her head to see out the window. Jackson ran through the snow with Lucky.

"He's magic? If he's pooping gold bricks, I want him back," he teased.

"He got Jackson to forget about video games for a while," she said. "I could never achieve that."

"That seems to be the way of it for kids today. Is that all he does?"

"He fools around with a guitar I bought him. I offered to get him lessons, but he said he enjoyed learning off of the internet—big surprise." She rose and popped a few slices of bread into the toaster. "Maybe I need to put my foot down. I'd love it if he committed to an instrument or a hobby. Maybe I should have gotten him a dog sooner."

"Stop second guessing yourself. You're a great mom." He knew a little something about moms. He'd had one too, but she was what they'd call a helicopter parent. A damn Military Apache Guardian. Quick and deadly. She saw everything. Knew everything. Her temper was like a heat-seeking missile. Never missed a thing except his unhappiness. He rather liked that Celia was more laid back and allowed Jackson to experience life organically.

"I hear that a lot, but I'm not fond of it."

He did a double take. "Being known as a great mom is a bad thing?"

"No, but it's usually followed by 'for someone so young.'"

"Not what I meant at all. Besides, you're not all that young to be a mom now." He tugged on her shirt to cover her shoulder. "Be careful, your chip is showing."

"You're right. I need to lighten up."

"On yourself for sure." He put his empty coffee cup in the sink. "I have to go. Thanks for the shelter, the company, the food—all of it." He lifted her hand and kissed it.

"Are you really going to have a conference call about developing the land?"

"Yes." he nodded. "I am."

That damn elephant took up residence in the room again, sitting heavily between them.

"It's a shame," she said.

"I'll touch base with you later. I would like for you to come see what I'm proposing. It might surprise you."

"What you're proposing will most likely put me out of business, Mr. McKenna."

"We're back to that?" he asked with frustration. "I've asked you to call me Rob."

"Okay, Rob. I have a brand and a reputation. My guests this weekend are coming all the way from Washington, D.C. to get away from it all. Future guests won't have that experience if you build your metropolis in my backyard. They'll bypass my place and go to yours."

"Come on, Celia, give it a chance."

"Have a good day." She walked to the front door and opened it for him. "Safe travels."

He slipped on his coat and headed outside. The snow was halfway up his calves as he stepped and sunk repeatedly to get to his truck.

Scott and his crew had done the worst job clearing him out. He climbed inside the cab and spied the man talking with Jackson. He rolled the truck toward them to hear the conversation.

"Tell your mom I have her materials loaded in the warehouse," Scott said. "They won't freeze that way."

"That's great," Rob broke in. "Maybe you can do that with my fencing. Can you keep it stored until the snow melts?"

"I'll look into it," Scott said stiffly.

"Maybe I should have had Celia ask you," teased Rob.

Jackson laughed hard, and by the red that painted Scott's face, it embarrassed him to have his crush called out. Scott marched to his Bobcat as quickly as he could.

"You nailed it, dude," said Jackson. "I think he has a creepy obsession for my mom."

"Make sure he doesn't hear you say that," counseled Rob with a smile.

"Yeah, not wise since Mom is on this Christmas committee with him."

"Christmas committee?" Rob cocked his head to the side.

"We have the Christmas Parade and people make these floats on old trailers. He's in charge of her material orders every year, and it's worse because this year Mom is making her own. I guess it wouldn't be a good idea to get on his bad side. But boy, it's obvious he likes her and doesn't care much for you."

Rob reached out and patted him on the shoulder. "I can't say as I blame him for liking your mom."

"Oh," said Jackson, getting the hint that Rob liked Celia too.

Rob put a finger to his lips. "Shh," he said. "Let's keep my secret crush between you and me."

"Got it," Jackson said.

"I gotta go. Lucky needs to get back inside."

"Why? He has fur."

"He does, but dogs get frostbite. Keep him off salted walkways and only have him come in and out until the snow melts."

"Okay." Jackson turned to walk away but pivoted around to face him. "When you're done with your work, can we play video games again?"

"Why don't you ask your mom if we can play online?" he said. "You can help me pick out a controller and maybe set me up. Probably not today, but if she says yes, we'll get started soon. How does that sound?"

"Sweet." The kid fist-pumped the air.

In giant strides, Jackson sailed back into the house with Lucky eagerly following. Celia came to the door and from across the yard they gazed at one another. What was that he saw in her eyes? Interest, or something less appealing like indifference?

CHAPTER NINE

CELIA

Being snowbound meant Celia got ahead in her preparation for her East Coast guests. She and Jackson made up the room Rob had used because it was the largest and had an attached bathroom. It was also the farthest from Jackson's, which sat above hers in the staff quarters. He liked his own space, and she didn't want to silence him when guests arrived.

"Where should I put Lucky? Rob still has his crate," he said as he was getting ready for work. "I can drive over and get it from him tomorrow, but that doesn't solve the problem for today."

"Lucky can stay with me. I'll put him in your room if I need to," she said. "Drive safely. The roads are clear, but that doesn't mean you can race around."

And with that, her son went out the door and Celia was alone.

She worked at her desk, searching the internet for Christmas float ideas. The parade was right around the corner. After the Harvest Festival, time would fly. It always did.

The festival was two weeks away and there was no doubt the crew was working at the Millers' indoor arena to build the stage for the performers. She appreciated the kindness of the Millers, who volunteered their horse arena every year.

After she finished her coffee, she set about doing her marketing. Celia put on her boots, coat, and earmuffs, and grabbed her camera to video the snow for her vlog. She walked around the grounds and took shots from the street and when she entered the house, the dog greeted her like he'd missed her with all his heart.

"I could get used to that, puppy." She dropped to her haunches to nuzzle his fur.

When she returned to her desk to upload her video, she had two emails that knocked the wind out of her. One notified her that the roof of the horse arena had collapsed under the weight of the snow. The other was her East Coast guests canceling their stay. There was nothing for her to do but weep. They'd withdrawn their reservation within the forty-eight-hour cancelation period, so she couldn't charge them anything. She had no defense against the gush of tears that erupted.

Celia cried so hard her eyes swelled.

She was glad Jackson was at work because she tried to insulate him from the hardships they faced. It wasn't just the cancelation. Or that she'd struggle to make her bills this month. It was everything, including how stirred up by Rob

McKenna she'd become. He reminded her of high school, and high school brought back memories of Jackson's dad.

Selfishly, she was happy her ex-husband wasn't around. Her son needed a dad, but Celia knew her ex would have never been the man Jackson needed. If he'd stayed, her poor boy would have been like her, chasing big Jackson for attention and affection and never receiving it.

At the moment, when finances were tight and business was dwindling, Celia wished she wasn't alone to handle everything by herself. That wasn't the case and would never be. It was all up to her.

She no longer had the luxury to fantasize about life being different. This was her reality.

After burying her head in her hands, she sobbed hard enough to make her stomach hurt. If she stretched out in her bed and covered herself with the goose down comforter, she could sleep forever, but that was an indulgence she couldn't afford.

She walked the dog into Jackson's room, made sure he had enough water and closed the door. As she shut it, a knock sounded at the door. She knew it was Scott. He'd come to tell her in person about the Miller arena. She wiped her face of the tears but didn't bother to hide that it upset her and walked toward the entrance.

"I already know, Scott," she said with resignation.

When she looked up, she saw Rob holding the crate. It folded up flat, but she knew what it was by the grated metal. Now she wished she'd washed her face.

"Jackson said he'd pick that up tomorrow." She turned her back to him and wiped under her eyes, hoping no old mascara stained her skin.

"My meeting finished early, and I thought I'd run it over. The snow is melting already, and the roads are clear."

He followed her inside and set the crate out of the way.

"The place looks amazing."

She looked at it through his eyes. There were special touches that hadn't been there earlier like flowers and bowls of wrapped chocolates.

He moved closer. "What's the matter?"

He shouldn't have asked her that. She wasn't sure she could control another round of tears if he pushed for an answer.

"Celia?"

She pointed behind her to the door, signaling him to leave. Her shoulders shook as the tears fell again. She controlled the sounds, but her body shook without reservation.

"Hey." He turned her toward him.

She pressed her forehead into his chest and let him put his arms around her. He smelled so damn good. He felt good too. The comfort of the contact with his body was exactly what she needed. She'd never experienced that with Jackson's dad.

Rob stroked her hair and told her everything would be okay while he held her.

"You want to talk?"

She shook her head but talked, anyway. "The arena where we hold our harvest festival collapsed."

Rob's chest rumbled with a chuckle. "Is that all? My goodness," he said. "They can find another place to hold the gathering."

"No, there isn't a place big enough." Her stomach twisted because she realized she had written a check on the money she thought she would make that weekend. It went against her better judgment, but Scott needed a down payment for the supplies before he would order them. Her body tensed and Rob pulled back. He lowered his face to hers, looking her straight in the eye.

"That isn't all of it, is it?"

"No," she rasped. "But I won't tell you the rest. Please go."

"Celia," he pleaded.

She pushed away. His touch, even if was just to comfort her, made her want things she couldn't have.

Having a guy like him around would be easy to get used to, but he was there to make his fortune and move on. He didn't understand what his small acts of kindness did to her. What they no doubt were doing to her son. He was giving them hope where hope shouldn't live.

"Bobby, I appreciate you bringing the crate over, but I'd appreciate it if you stopped going out of your way. Jackson would have been there tomorrow."

"Please don't call me Bobby."

She took in a big breath. "Please just go. I have things to do." Her words came out sounding hollow for the lies they were.

She needed him to leave so she could go to the hardware store. Maybe Scott hadn't put her check through to the bank for the Christmas Parade materials. The plan was for her to cover the expenses from her business account and have the members pay back their share. Now that she was in a jam, she wondered why that had ever been a rational idea.

"See yourself out," she said in a rush. "Thanks for the crate."

She hurried back to her apartment and made sure she left nothing on. The dog was secured, and she bundled up for the cold weather and grabbed her keys. Celia raised the garage door and counted her blessings if for no other reason than to calm herself down.

She rolled her car back and got all the way out to the end of the drive to realize there were piles of snow blocking her view. She inched back and crossed her fingers she wouldn't get T-boned. The whole situation made her snap. She lost it, yelling her head off like a crazy woman. "Why does the universe hate me?" She looked up and screamed. She pounded on the steering wheel.

When she made it onto the road, she paused and took a breath. Rob was still there. He had parked his truck in a space between the piles of snow. He had his cellphone in his hand like he'd been checking emails or sending a text or something, but he watched her. No doubt, he'd seen her flip out.

Celia rolled down the window. "Why are you here? I asked you to go."

"Working on it." He tucked his phone inside his pocket and took a step toward her. "You okay there?"

She hated to be horrid to him, but she needed to protect her son and her heart. Better to not have Rob at all than have him abandon her down the road. "We're not your responsibility," she said. "Jackson and I were fine before you came, and we'll be fine after you leave."

"We'll talk later, Celia."

"There's no need," she said, grasping for control of something—anything.

She felt like a child throwing a tantrum, but she'd lost control of her emotions, of her finances, and of her feelings for him. Since she couldn't get a handle on the first two, she had to make sure she put him out of her life. Problems filled her plate. She didn't need to add man trouble to the list.

She rolled her window up and navigated the short, slushy distance to the hardware store. It wouldn't serve her well if she unleashed her foul mood on Scott. She had to play nice with the man who scraped at her nerves.

As soon as she stepped inside Pinetop Hardware, Scott was on her like an ant to sticky candy. She hoped this time it was because he had a thing for her and not because he had to speak to her about a bounced check.

"Celia," he greeted her curtly.

The last thing she needed was to deal with an attitude. Her guess was it didn't make him happy to see Rob around.

She smiled and greeted him warmly.

"Thanks again for clearing the driveway. Unfortunately, my reservations canceled this morning, but it's nice to have it done." She hoped that would garner her sympathy.

"Sorry to hear that."

"I only mention it because I wrote a check for the materials. If you still have that, I'd appreciate it if we could hold off depositing it."

He eyed her with suspicion. "You're welcome to cover it on credit if that works better for you."

She let out the breath she'd been holding. "That would be a lifesaver." She hoped the relief showed in the smile she forced to her lips.

A genuine smile would have been nice if she could muster it, but it wasn't possible despite his answer being the best thing to happen all morning.

"Your hands must be full with the Miller Arena. I don't know what will happen with the festival given the circumstances. It's not like we can hold it here or anything," she said, looking at the store and thinking it would be the perfect building if it were empty.

"The problem is solved," he said with a tone of disappointment. "I'm surprised you didn't know."

"What do you mean?" She was at a loss.

"Your guest from this morning saved the day." He forced the same fake smile she'd given him.

Celia staggered back. She'd just yelled at Rob.

"How did he do that?"

"He's erecting a prefabricated structure on his land. He bought a barn he'll put up in a day. It was no big deal since he said it would convert to something else when he developed the property. For now, we have a place for the festival." He clapped his hands together like he was wiping something away. "Problem solved. There won't even be a need to move the date."

Celia blinked. Tears stung her eyes, and she didn't want Scott to see her get emotional.

"That works out great then. Now, if I can get someone to come stay at my inn, it would be a fantastic day." She gave him a backward wave goodbye. "Thanks, Scott. I guess that's it then."

"Celia?"

She spun around when he called her.

"Yes?"

"Is that all you came here for?" He shoved his hands inside his pockets. "To talk about the account?"

"Yes." She didn't know where he was going with the question.

"You could have called. Did you think it would work better if you asked me in person?"

She knew he was accusing her of playing him.

"I thought it was better to face you since it wasn't a casual request. It was a big deal."

"Sure." He cocked his head sideways. "Did you ask Rob McKenna to buy that barn for you?"

"No. I didn't." It occurred to her that Scott might have thought she'd slept her way to a venue. Why would she do that? The festival wasn't even her thing. "Not that it's any of your business, but he gave us his mother's dog last night and got caught in the storm. He and Jackson played computer games until the wee hours. We aren't a thing." It hurt her to admit that. What would being a thing with Rob McKenna be like?

Scott smiled with what she thought was relief.

"Hey, I appreciate you coming out in the snow and all and meeting with me. I didn't mean—" he started to say.

She'd had enough of him, so she didn't let him finish.

"Yes, you did, but that's okay. I think we're clear now. Talk to you later."

All she could think about as she hurried back to her car was Rob bought a barn, and she had mistreated him. She had to find a way to make that up to him.

CHAPTER TEN

ROB

During a video conference with his resort designer, Rob decided on a community of small but modern bungalows, all of them prefabricated. The construction of the resort would be a matter of grading the land, installing utilities, and putting in roads.

Once Pinetop was on board, and the permits department okayed his plans, his property could be developed quickly.

He threw so much business toward Sand Creek Construction that it was easy to talk them into prioritizing the building of the new barn. He wasn't sure what he'd do with it once the festival was over, but he considered selling it to the Millers or working it into the design of the resort. Either way, it wasn't a loss.

He was quick to solve the problem because he had a thing for Celia, but he hadn't thought it through. He should have waited. Maybe asked her. He just did what he did. Her rejection stung worse because he wasn't one to fall easily and hated that he didn't know how to move forward with his growing feelings for her.

It didn't help that he opened his door to find Jackson. He was another piece of the puzzle that was confusing. He wasn't expecting to like him as much as he did. They say a way to a man's heart is through his stomach, but that's bull. Put a beautiful woman who needs love and her son who needs a role model in his path and his heart was all in.

"Hey, Jackson," Rob said.

The sight of him made Rob's chest expand with pride. Not because he had anything to do with Jackson's upbringing, but because Celia had raised such a good kid with a big heart and a wonderful personality.

"Hi," he replied.

"What can I do for you?"

Jackson looked at him like he was speaking in tongues. "I'm here to pick up the crate."

Rob cocked his head like Lucky did when anyone spoke to the dog. "I delivered that yesterday." He made sure not to sound impatient or rude. Jackson had enough of that behavior from his father.

The boy stepped forward like he wanted to come inside the house, but Rob didn't invite him in because Celia had asked him to stay away from her son.

"Where did you put it?" Poor Jackson looked confused.

"I gave it to your mom," he said. "I walked it into the house. It's folded up so maybe you didn't know what it was."

"Huh, weird." He scratched his head. "I mentioned I was coming over here to get it, but Mom said nothing. Maybe it's because she's not feeling great."

"She's sick?" he asked with concern. "What's wrong?"

He shouldn't get involved. She told him to stay away from her and Jackson, but he couldn't help himself.

"I don't know. She wants to ask you over to dinner soon, so maybe you can talk to her then." He looked at his phone. "I'm supposed to drive her to the grocery store in a little while, so she must feel better. She spent all day yesterday and most of this morning in bed." Jackson frowned. "It's not like her, so it had to have been a bug."

"Okay, well, I hope she's better. Let me know when she wants to have dinner." His head spun. One moment she told him to leave her alone and the next she was planning dinner.

"Most likely this weekend since her booking canceled."

Rob's head whipped to attention. "But you guys worked so hard on the house."

"I know, right? That was a huge reservation. They were staying for a week. Now she has a lot of time on her hands."

"Why don't we do this," Rob began. "If she's not feeling well, we can handle dinner. Maybe we could take her out?"

"Yeah, I guess we could." He shoved his hands in his pockets and shuffled back and forth. "To be honest, she'd be happier eating at home. She's not too keen on the local restaurants."

"You could come here," Rob offered. "I have a great kitchen, with a flame broil grill, and the dining room has a cool view. I'll take you grocery shopping and we could surprise her."

"She would go for that."

"It's a secret though. I don't want to shake her up too much, but let's do something nice for your mom. What do you like to eat?"

"Hamburgers." The word popped out like he'd been holding it in for a lifetime.

Rob laughed. "Surprise. A Colorado lad likes beef. I should have asked what your mother likes to eat?"

"She likes beef, chicken. Salad. Any kind of salad and she's there. She's easy to please."

Rob would have loved to argue that point, but he didn't. "Can we pull this off?"

"I have to take her to the store," he said. "I'm not sure if I can go with you."

"Why is that?" he asked.

"Because I promised her, and if we're going to make it a surprise, then everything has to seem normal."

"You can't make up an excuse? What kind of sixteen-year-old are you if you can't snow your mother?"

"I never lie to her," he said with dead seriousness. "My dad did all the time, and it's not cool."

It blew Rob away. "I never meant to suggest—"

Jackson amended his answer. "I tell her everything, but I'm working on something for her for Christmas, so I guess there are some things I keep to myself."

"Really? What are you getting her?"

"Not telling." He grinned.

"Well, whatever I do for dinner will be like that," said Rob. "Like a Christmas present. A nice surprise. I'll handle it. Text me whatever else you want for dinner, and I'll pick it up."

They parted ways. He would go to the store by himself, but first, he called his designer.

"Alex, I need you."

"Hey buddy, you're a good-looking guy but not my type."

"Don't be an ass. I need a favor." Rob paced his entryway.

"What's up?" he asked.

"I want you to rent a room at the Hummingbird Inn. Book it for a week and then cancel at the last minute. I'll pay for everything."

"Why?"

"It's for a friend, and she can't know."

"*She?*" he asked. "Why not just buy her flowers or chocolate? It's cheaper."

"Or you can come out. That might be better. You can see the land firsthand. I'll still pay for everything. Bring your girlfriend."

"Do you hear how nuts you sound?" Alex chuckled into the phone. "I'll see if Nicole wants to come. Let me call you back." There was a moment of silence. "Hey, what if she's booked by the time I have my answer?"

"Then book her next available opening." Rob smiled to himself. He knew she didn't want his interference, but he also knew she couldn't afford a vacancy.

"And we aren't using your credit card because you don't want her to know you're giving her business because you want to give her the business, right?"

"Very mature, Alex." Rob shook his head. "I'll reimburse you. Grow up, man."

"Never, but I'll text you when it's all set. If we come out, can I let her know who we are to you? I mean won't she know, eventually?"

"I'll just pretend it's a coincidence. Do your part, and I'll handle the rest."

As he headed out the door and climbed into his truck, he realized he missed having Lucky around. It was the darnedest thing, but he would have liked to have the dog at the grocery store with him.

The dinner menu ran through his head as he drove into town. Gourmet burgers, seasoned fries, and a salad sounded good.

The town wasn't far away from his house and it reminded him of how Celia said everything he needed was here. She could very well be right. Even if there was no industry or money flowing through it, Pinetop had its own kind of perfection.

Each time he entered the grocery store, the small-town charm moved him. Its shiny, waxed linoleum floors and pristine, crisp aisles with neatly stacked displays evoked a safe and bountiful experience.

He understood why people put down roots in a place like this. It was more than a town. It was a community. That was something he hadn't been part of for a while.

He started at one end of the store and worked his way around. When his cart filled, he rounded the aisle heading to the checkout and came face to face with Celia and Jackson. They'd caught him.

"Hello," he said awkwardly.

He and Celia had parted on brittle terms, which made running into her feel awkward. She was the mother of a teenager who with any hope and luck would be in college in two years. And yet, the figure she cut in a sweet, rose-colored sweater and dark blue straight-legged jeans which she'd tucked into riding-style boots established that she was young and vibrant. The girl he'd had a crush on in high school had become a beautiful woman.

"Hello." She lowered her head.

He wondered, if she looked at him, would he see happiness or frustration?

"I have to go to work," Jackson said. "Later, Rob." He kissed his mom's cheek and disappeared down the next aisle.

"I'm glad I ran into you." Celia lifted her head and smiled, and his world became a better place because of it.

He arched a brow. "Are you?" His gentle scold made her blush.

"I want to apologize for losing it the other day."

He wouldn't gloss it over and say it was fine, not quickly anyway.

"Okay." He needed to say more so she would know he was there for her. "I know it seems as if we've just met, but we haven't, have we? You can always let me know what's going on."

"Yeah, I mean, no." She buried her face in her hands. "It was a terrible moment."

"I hope it passed." He wanted to touch her, to pull her close to him for a hug, but he gave her the space he thought she needed.

"It has, but that's not what I wanted to talk to you about." She took a step closer. "Thank you for offering your place for the festival. That was generous."

"It's my pleasure."

They stared at each other for a long moment.

He took great pleasure in the way her sweet lips formed an O.

"Jackson and I would like to invite you to dinner." It was like a string got pulled from above to hoist her up. She grew two inches in the last couple of minutes. "Our way of saying thanks for the venue and to make up for the way I snapped at you."

Her eyes pleaded with him to say yes, but that wasn't the plan.

"I'll tell you what. It's my turn to host a dinner, and what I'd enjoy is having you at my place. I'm already shopping, and we can pick out anything else you'd like to make together."

Celia looked at his selections with confusion.

"Do you always shop for yourself like that?" She pointed to the items in his full cart. "Looks fancy."

It looked like a dinner party in the making.

"I broke the rule about shopping while hungry." He picked up a package of beef. "I have to have this ground by the butcher. Come with me."

He liked the feel of walking with her. Suddenly, a loud ring broke the silence and drowned out the soft tunes playing on the store's sound system. He turned to Celia, who scrambled to get her phone out of her bag.

"I got an email." She checked her phone and gasped.

"Oh my gosh." She held her cell in the air and waved it around. "I have someone interested in the inn for this weekend."

"But you're booked," he said, pretending he didn't know about the cancellation.

The joy and light in her face made the lie worth it if the email was from Alex.

"My booking canceled because of the snow." She stopped and stared at him. "Wait, this guy says he works for you."

Alex telling her right away was off-script—it should have come later—but Rob went with it.

"Wait." He acted shocked, though most of it was genuine. He took the phone from her. "Did he book with you? I told him he could stay with me."

"Oh," she said. "It's okay if you'd rather they stay with you. It's fine. It looks like he's bringing a companion."

Rob realized the brilliance of Alex's disclosure. It sort of got him off the hook for fibbing to her. This way it was legitimate. The next problem was answering why he'd fly his designer out to look at land covered with snow. He'd figure that out later.

"No." Rob handed her back her phone. "If he wants to stay at your place, that's fine with me. Perfect actually."

"Are you sure you don't mind?"

"Not in the least."

"That means we have to have dinner tonight." She glanced toward the registers. "But Jackson's working."

A tingling sensation washed through him at the possibility of having dinner alone with her. As much as he liked Jackson, alone time with Celia sounded wonderful.

"Do you think we can handle that?" he asked, winking at her.

"Yeah," she sighed. "But we took one car here, so I'll come back and pick him up."

"Why don't you leave the keys with him and ride home with me? We can stop and put your things away, or you can keep them in my fridge. I'm a big boy, I know how to share."

"Great plan." Her expression brightened. "I can't believe I got a replacement booking." She hopped up and down like a kid.

"It is awesome." Rob put his arm around her. It seemed like the most natural thing to do. He gazed down on her sweet face while they walked through the store.

"Shall we have wine?"

"Definitely." Her eyes focused on him. "And something naughty for dessert."

CHAPTER ELEVEN

CELIA

Aton of weight lifted from her shoulders as she walked around the store with Rob. She wished she was better dressed because it felt like a date.

He handed the butcher the steaks to grind up while they waited.

"Jackson said he liked burgers. I figured I'd get these ground up."

"Wait a minute." Her eyes snapped to his. "Why would you be doing burgers for Jackson?"

Rob's face turned red. "He mentioned it and I—"

"But you asked us to dinner just now." She glanced down at his cart. "You already had everything in your cart, and he's not coming."

"Jackson gave me the idea when he came for the crate."

"You sure go fancy on your burgers." She never ground up a good steak. She bought the 80/20 ground beef when it was on sale.

"I like high-quality ingredients. If I put in the effort, I want it to be worthwhile. Where is this going? Do you have a problem with me making you dinner or is everything still good?"

"Umm ... it's good."

Maybe it was the anxiety she'd endured for the past forty-eight hours that caused her radar to go up for a moment. After the stress she put herself through, she refused to ruin the night by flying off the handle again.

They walked their carts up to check out. Jackson was at the register, so they went to his line. She pulled his car keys out of her purse and handed them over.

"Rob will give me a ride home." She loved the sound of that. She realized then she had not allowed herself to miss the company of a man, even if it was just a casual acquaintance. However, this dinner with Rob didn't feel casual, and she didn't feel like an acquaintance. There had been something stirring between them since the day he knocked on her door.

"Sweet," said Jackson.

She always looked at her balance when she checked out, but this time it mortified her. Scott said he would put the supplies on credit and not send her check through, but he hadn't kept his word, and now she didn't have enough in her account to cover the groceries.

Rob reached around her to her son, handing him a bank card. He was offering to buy their groceries too. She didn't understand why, but she had to swallow her pride and let him.

"You don't have to do that."

"Aren't those for your guests this weekend?"

"Mostly," she said.

"Let me do this for you."

He stared into her eyes and she soaked it up. His eyes were one of the many things that drew her to him. Blue eyes that sparkled with bits of sunshine-colored flecks thrown in.

"Did you see my bank account balance just now?" She was embarrassed, but he didn't make a big deal out of it.

He was quiet for a moment. "Yes," he said.

Their bodies were so near she felt a pulse wavering between them. The arc of energy that passed from him to her and back again made her insides stir with heat as if the crackling had breached her skin.

"Thought so," she grumbled. "How humiliating."

"It happens," he whispered.

It felt like they were the only two people in Pinetop at that moment. The blood rushed to her ears and blocked all sounds and senses except for the sight and feel of him.

"Do you make it a habit to rescue a damsel in distress?" she flirted.

"Yep, if her name is Celia Roberts, I do," he said. "Let's go have dinner."

"Declined," said Jackson of Rob's credit card.

Celia and Rob jerked their heads in his direction while Jackson laughed his head off.

"Just kidding," he said. "Woke you up though."

Rob laughed hard.

Celia felt like she had just survived the drop of a roller coaster.

"You wait," she warned her son. "I'll get you back for that."

The snow from the last few days had melted, and the temperature had risen into the high thirties.

Rob lifted his groceries into the back of his truck. Celia tried to do the same, but at just over five feet, she wasn't tall enough. He stood behind her and lifted them for her, putting his arms around her. She hadn't felt anything so amazing in a lifetime.

He opened the passenger door for her like the gentleman he was proving to be. She raised her leg, but her jeans didn't have enough give, so the height of the truck was a challenge. After a failed attempt, he lifted her at the waist and set her on the passenger seat.

"That was easy," she said. It was an understatement. Everything about Rob was easy except for him developing the land behind her home. She'd gotten used to the idea that it was going to happen. The harder pill to swallow was that it would put her out of business. She and Jackson were just making ends meet. How could she raise a teenage boy without an income? She'd had to separate the man from the land, or it would ruin the evening.

Rob climbed into the driver's seat and was about to turn onto the road but stopped.

"Was that what upset you the other day? Did you forget your account was overdrawn?"

She shook her head. "It shouldn't have been. Scott promised to hold a check and transfer the money I owed to credit, and he didn't."

He flashed an artificial smile. "You don't have to rely on Scott anymore. You can rely on me."

"But why?" she asked.

"Why not?" he countered.

"I've made it a rule to not allow myself to rely on anyone. I don't want to be foolish."

"You're not foolish, and you have to trust someone sometime. Why not me?"

He leaned over and kissed her.

To her surprise, she kissed him back. She leaned into him, running her fingers through his thick, dark hair. After a long, languorous kiss, she stilled.

"You kissed me," she said.

He chuckled. "And you kissed me back."

"I did," she whispered against his lips. "We'll be the talk of the town."

He curled his lips into a smile. One that revealed a hidden dimple. If she wasn't already smitten with the man, that dimple would do it.

"Let them talk. Maybe good ole Scott will put your check through a second time out of spite."

"Wouldn't put it past him."

"I hope they talk about this," he said. "I've been fantasizing about having my name linked to you ever since your boyfriend pants'd me in high school."

"Oh man," she said, and she pressed her forehead to his chest. "I'm so sorry."

He leaned back and winked. "Jackson never did it again because he didn't want you looking at my junk."

"He didn't want me looking at anything." She nuzzled against him and breathed him in. "He was so mean."

"And yet, you liked him." He leaned away and arched a brow.

"I did, but only God knows why." She sat back and adjusted the seatbelt. "Once you got past his good looks, there wasn't much there. I'm so glad Jackson is nothing like him."

"He looks like you, and he's sweet like you." Rob started the truck and turned onto the highway toward his house. "I'm glad, too, because it would be hard to deal with a mini Jackson every day of your life."

"You're right." She turned to look at him. "Do you look like your father?" It just dawned on her that his father was never around.

"Spitting image and my mother hated me for it."

She reached over and took his hand. "I'm so sorry, Rob. It's not your fault."

"Not everyone has a heart of gold like you do."

"Is that why you left town right after graduation?"

"Yep, tired of my mom hovering over me so I'd never turn out like him. If I didn't know better, I'd say Jackson Sr. and my father were cut from the same cloth."

She remembered the day Jackson came home with a bipolar diagnosis. He threw the meds across the room and stomped out the door. He left for months that time.

"Was your father mentally ill too?"

"No, mine was selfish and self-centered."

They pulled into his driveway and brought the bags inside.

"Did I miss this behemoth refrigerator the last time I was here?" She opened and closed the door several times. "I could book this as a room at the inn."

"You should have one of these."

"I'm going for authentic. I don't think they had these in Victorian homes."

"They didn't have air conditioning or central heating or remote-control lighting either. They had boxes with ice. Is that what you're using?"

She could lie to herself all she wanted. Her inn might look Victorian, but it had most of the amenities expected in the 21st century. "No, I'm more modern than that."

He flipped a remote, and the air filled with soft jazz.

"You know how to live," she said.

"Glad you like it." He poured a glass of red wine from a bottle he had tucked against the backsplash and handed it to her.

He washed his hands and formed the patties from the ground sirloin and set them on the grill. While those sizzled, he washed up again and took one of her hands in his. He placed his other hand on the small of her back and moved around the room to the beat of the music.

How long had it been since she'd danced with someone? When was the last time her heartbeat took off like a gazelle chased by a lion? For the first time in a long time, her senses came alive.

"I haven't danced since high school." This was unfamiliar territory. She'd been a mother for the last sixteen years and had forgotten how to dance. She'd forgotten how to be a woman.

A strange look came over his face.

"You didn't dance at your wedding?"

"We didn't have a wedding." Her heart ached as if a fist were gripping it. It wasn't because there wasn't a white dress or a reception, or because she didn't dance. It was because her marriage started past the finish line. "Our parents took us to get married at the courthouse in the next county over. We signed some papers, and that was it. I was pregnant and Jackson was miserable. The grownup me feels sorry for him. We had no business getting married. We weren't in love."

He put a finger to her lips. "Not your fault." He drew her in until she fell into his arms. He tilted his head to the side and whispered, "I'm going to kiss you again."

"Don't tell me, just do it."

His lips brushed against hers in a slow, sensuous sweep. Never had she been kissed in a way that made her knees weak. Emotionally starved, this was the affection she had longed for her entire life.

Their bodies barely moved as they pressed together. They tasted, and touched, and experienced each other in the most organic, free-flowing way. Their breaths mingled, whispering words neither could understand but somehow understood.

A timer dinged, interrupting the moment.

"I gotta flip the burgers," he growled.

He let go so he could tend to their meal.

Celia smoothed her hair and ran her fingers over her kiss-swollen lips. She wanted to tell him to leave the burgers because she wasn't hungry for food but starving for him.

"What about you?" She walked over and leaned on the counter. "Has there been anyone in your life since high school?" She held her breath, waiting for his answer.

"There have been a few trials and errors, but I'm afraid business has been my lady love."

"Does she love you back?" She understood where he was coming from. She was married to her work too. Only for her, it was a way to survive. She got the feeling that for him it went deeper.

"She's been kind, but she doesn't fill my bed at night."

"What do you do exactly?"

"I make deals and develop properties." He topped off her wine, then leaned on the counter and watched over the pan. "It had been things like strip malls and office buildings, but those are becoming a thing of the past. It's an exercise in ingenuity to hunt down new deals."

"Is that why you're thinking about developing here?" She knew why. A large chunk of property had landed in his lap. When a cook gets a lobster he boils, broils, or barbecues it. When Rob gets land, he develops it. "Is it because it's new or because you have nothing better to do?"

He let go of a full, genuine laugh.

She loved the way he looked when he smiled and let loose. Seeing his grin could almost make her forget his intention to destroy her life.

"My mother didn't know what to do with it. I know she left it to me because I do. It'll be good, you'll see. The process will be quick and painless once we get the plans approved. Contrary to your beliefs, it will mean more business for you."

"No," she said, shaking her head. "That's not possible. Who will want to stay in a cutesy Victorian inn when they can have a shiny new place with fake snow and room service?"

"We can talk about this later." He tugged her by a belt loop toward him. "My designer is coming into town, and you're invited to join in the discussions. I want your input because you know Pinetop better than I do."

He gave her a quick kiss and averted his attention back to the pan.

"Dinner is ready."

"You're changing the subject, Mr. McKenna."

"I am." He winked.

ROB

"Come," he said as he took their plates and walked into the great room to sit at the table in front of the window.

"And this is where any likeness to the Victorian era home ends." She'd picked up the wine and their glasses and set them on the table.

"Are you disappointed?" He put their plates on the side facing the view. "That's the beauty of the company I work with. You can mix and match." He was a fan of great rooms. It made the space open and less claustrophobic. Victorians were compartmentalized, with rooms designed for specific needs. The parlor, the music room, the conservatory. That was fine too, but after a lifetime of living in a house that left him needing space and room to grow, he loved having a wide-open area.

"But your mom's house is a true Victorian, and it's yours."

He drew out the chair next to his so she could sit, eat, and enjoy nature at its best. Soon the blanket of night would fall over the land and they would see nothing but a dark sky and a kaleidoscope of stars.

"I like the look of the old, but with modern amenities. You don't find that in older homes or old towns like Pinetop."

"What's wrong with Pinetop?"

"Nothing," he said. "People love quaint towns. I consider it a selling point for the resort. A resort that will create jobs for the people here. Have you considered that this might be a good thing?"

She nodded. "I have." She sipped her wine. "What did you do with your mom's house?"

He smiled. "Are you interested, Miss Roberts?" He turned the tables on her by calling her by her last name as she did him.

"You mean like another inn?"

"Or maybe dividing it into apartments. There are many options, but it needs a lot of work."

He spied on their reflection in the window. They both struggled to focus on their meals. That kiss changed everything. It was filled with hope, and want, and desire. They turned to each other and appeared to have the same thing on their minds—no doubt another kiss.

Leaning forward, they drew together like magnets. He leaned down as she looked up. When their lips pressed together all inhibition and caution disappeared.

She shifted and moved from her chair to straddle him. She wrapped her arms around his neck and kissed him as if it would be the last kiss of a lifetime. If he had anything to do with it, it would be the first kiss of the rest of her life.

Touching, licking, stroking. They moved against each other until neither could catch their breath. He pulled back and lifted his eyes to meet hers. His expression relayed the message he wanted so much more, but was that wise?

Rob stood with his hands cradling her bottom and walked her to the sofa where he plopped down on the cushions. When they settled in, she straddled him once more.

Their plates went untouched because a more demanding hunger had to be sated. He flipped the remote and lit the fireplace to set the mood. His eager lips brushed against the curve of her neck, tasting her skin with the tip of his tongue. He nibbled and suckled while she shivered and dug her nails into his upper arms.

Against her skin, he murmured, "Like that?"

"Yes." Her breath came out whisper soft.

She took his hand and slipped it under her sweater.

His palm cupped her breast before his fingers explored what she offered.

Lifting her sweater over her head, he tossed it aside. He needed to touch her and taste her. Hell, he wanted to devour her.

The moan that burst from her mouth made it more perfect.

She was timid but steady in her exploration of him. Her touch was light as she stroked his shoulders and down his arms.

When her hands grazed his thighs, drawing the tips of her nails across the denim, her touch sent sparks of energy pulsing through him. His breath was labored, and his head clouded with passion, and they hadn't even gotten to the good stuff.

He didn't want to rush the moment, but he was impatient. He leaned her back on the couch and gazed at her. The satin cups of her bra pushed beneath her breasts, lifting them like an offering.

He pulled back, bringing everything to a screeching halt. This all happened so fast and while he was eager to continue, it was important to make sure everything was perfect for her.

She rose to her elbows. "What's wrong?"

"I got carried away." He ran his fingers through his hair as if the seconds that passed would lessen his desire. One look at Celia and he knew he'd want her always.

"I thought getting carried away was the point. Is something wrong?"

"No," he said with a soft laugh. "It's very right. Are you sure about this? Are you ready to take this to the next level?"

"I know what this is, Rob." Her hands moved under his shirt —the burning so intense he would have sworn her fingertips were high voltage. "You don't have to be chivalrous. I'm a grown woman."

He took in her body from those soulful eyes to the button of her jeans.

"No argument there." He tucked his fingers under her waistband. "I just want to do right by you."

"Then take me upstairs," she whispered.

And with that, he carried her to his bedroom. He laid her down in the middle of the mattress with the bedding fluffed around her.

Celia propped herself up on her elbows and watched him strip. "No wonder Jackson never pants'd you again. He felt inadequate."

"One more chance to change your mind. I don't want you to regret this."

She gave him another once-over. "My only regret will be if you stop. Just once I'd love to have sex because I want it. A moment where my body screams louder than my mind. A chance to know what this connection between us will feel like if we let it take over. Give me that. I won't ask for anything else."

He reached for the waist of her jeans. With the skill of a magician, her clothes disappeared in seconds.

Her amusement and carefree laugh touched him.

She'd had such a brilliant smile in high school. Those in his small, humble group of unpopular boys who worshiped her from afar referred to her as Miss Colgate because she had perfectly white, straight teeth. He was glad he could bring a smile back to her face.

"You're so beautiful."

"You're not so bad yourself." She tugged on his shoulders, so he moved closer.

She kissed him, her tongue slipping into his mouth to release a floodgate of desire. Heat gathered in the pit of his stomach. Could a man burn to be inside a woman?

She took his face in her delicate hands. "I want this. I need this."

He positioned himself between her welcoming thighs and lowered his mouth to hers before he pressed into her body.

Celia moved with him, moaning with each stroke. Several minutes later, he rolled onto his back, swinging her above him. She pressed her palms to his chest. Gone was the demure, hesitant single mother, and in her place was a fiery siren. The sight of her uninhibited and taking what she needed drove him wild.

"You keep that up, and I won't last," he groaned.

Her eyes sparkled with mischief. "We'll just have to go for round two."

"I'm all in." He strained against his release, waiting for her to catch up to him. She kept a steady pace while he touched her in the place that would undo her.

She opened her mouth, her eyes fluttered, and then what started as tiny spasms grew into a tight fist that clenched around his length until he gave in and rode out his release.

They were a tangle of limbs, spent and gasping for air.

"I've never—"

"That's not true," he teased.

"Never like that." She curled into his chest.

"That's how it should always be." He kissed the top of her head and held her tight. He'd had plenty of good sex, but he'd had nothing like he'd experienced with Celia. Far more than their sex organs connected them. Their hearts linked them together.

She thought she knew what this was. No doubt she considered it a one-night stand, but she was wrong. This was more. This was everything.

CHAPTER THIRTEEN

CELIA

She woke and bolted upright. "What time is it?"

He checked his watch. "It's only eleven. It seems later than it is. Do you need to get going?"

"Yeah." She rolled out of bed and gathered her clothes. "Jackson will be home. What will he think? I've never been out like this before."

One look at Rob and she debated between being a selfish lover and a good mom. How much she wanted to climb back in bed and let him make her feel again.

"What time does the store close?"

"It closes at ten, and he stays after to stock for the next day. If we hurry, I'll be home when he gets home."

Rob got up and slipped into his jeans.

Celia yanked her pants up and almost toppled over.

"Hey." He stopped her. "You'll be there at the same time. He knows you're over at my house for dinner. It's okay."

"I've never been out with—" she began.

"With a man, you mean," he finished for her. "Is that what this is about? Is this about your son or you?"

"I don't know what you mean." She tugged on her shoes and looked around for her sweater.

"It's okay to take time for yourself, Celia. Relax. We'll get you home in time," he assured her. "Your sweater is by the couch."

He was so perceptive. Part of what made her squirrelly was feeling like a naughty teenager, but it wouldn't be her parents catching her sneaking in, but her son. How frustrating was it to have one of the best moments of her life and not allow herself to enjoy it?

"I know. This is all new to me," she whispered.

"Then we'll practice so it becomes second nature. You'll be a pro in no time."

They rushed downstairs, where she tugged on her sweater, grabbed her groceries and headed out the door.

"I'm sorry to leave you with the mess."

He reached over and held her hand. "Isn't it time someone else got the mess? Looks to me like you've been dealing with it long enough."

They remained silent for the few minutes it took to get to her house.

At her door, he kissed her goodbye.

"I'll call you tomorrow," she promised.

SEVERAL DAYS PASSED since their amazing night. Rob texted her, and she ignored him. Tension coiled in her stomach. She couldn't figure it out. Rob was the whole package. He was handsome, self-made, generous, and he liked her son. They shared a history, and he made her feel things she'd never felt in her life—things only found in books and movies.

She ran scared because she knew what their time was—one night and nothing more. She tried to live her life as a realist and Rob McKenna was out of her league.

So much time had passed since their intimate encounter, and the pause gave her a moment to think. Those thoughts stirred up deep-seated feelings that weren't good. Rob would eventually leave, and she couldn't stand to be abandoned again, so she'd sabotaged everything.

She did her best to maintain a clear head for Jackson. He was an independent kid, but she was glad he still needed things like a lunch and an occasional hug. Those small things made her feel necessary.

As soon as he was out the door to school, she was alone, but her mind wasn't silent. Her thoughts were there chattering away.

It was years ago, and she still felt abandoned by Jackson Sr. It wasn't as if she wanted him back; she wanted to be needed, and he didn't need her, nor did he want her. That was why the small things she could do for her son made her feel good, like somehow her contribution to his life brought value.

She didn't have time to wallow in insecurities. Her weekend guests would arrive before Jackson got home from school.

She hoped they would touch base and then be out the door. She'd be here to greet them and give them a rundown of the place and then retreat into her apartment for the weekend. Maybe with some leftover Halloween chocolate, a pint of ice cream, or a box of Little Debbie snacks. Not a little box but an economy pack.

ALEX AND HIS GIRLFRIEND, Nicole, arrived on time. She escorted them to their rooms and showed them where the bathroom was. She told them they could help themselves to the refrigerator and figured that would be it.

"We thought we could get dinner," Alex said. "I read that dinner was available for a fee."

He pointed to a brochure he'd saved on his phone. She offered meals if the guests requested the service ahead of time. She didn't feel like doing anything but disappearing into her place and hiding, but they'd rescued her from the cancellation, and she felt obligated.

As nice as she could, she said, "Normally, I'd require advance notice, but I can cook for you if you'd like."

"Anything you make will be fantastic," Alex said. "I'll give Rob a call and let him know we're here. I'd want him to join us."

"Rob?" she asked, knowing perfectly well who he was talking about.

"Yes." Nicole looked at Alex. "Didn't he say this would be a great place to rent? I can tell you, we're in love with it already. It's cute and comfortable."

Alex gave Nicole a look that could wilt a flower.

"Rob suggested it to you?" She was at odds with her feelings for him. She'd wanted that night as badly as he did, but she hadn't considered the repercussions. He wasn't here long term. He was in town to make money and leave. It was the leaving part that made her feel foolish because she'd set herself up for heartbreak.

"He might have mentioned the place," Alex said.

That didn't quite match up with the story Rob had told her. The discrepancy made things stranger. As much as she tried to convince herself he differed from Jackson's father, the fibs sounded familiar. When he arrived, would he be honest?

"I can do salmon fillets with lemon butter sauce, grilled broccoli, and couscous. Does that work?"

"Sounds great," Nicole said. "We'll unpack and touch base with Rob."

As Celia set about preparing the food, she scoured her brain to remember exactly how it went—whether Rob acted like it was a coincidence that his colleagues chose her, or whether he said he'd recommended her inn. She thought he'd invited them to his place, and they'd declined. Rather than dwell on it, she sent a text to Jackson.

Hi. I'm making salmon for our guests. Do you want any?

He responded with lightning speed.

No thanks. I'll pick up frozen burgers here.

She wanted to ask him if he'd mentioned the cancellation to Rob but decided against involving him.

On that note, Lucky bounded toward her. She had forgotten to put him in his crate, and he nosed his way out of the apartment.

"Come on, boy," she said in a sweet voice. She put the salmon fillets in a bowl of warm water to thaw and preheated the oven before she let him out back to romp around the yard. Celia drew back the curtains to monitor him.

Nicole came downstairs and froze. "Is that a dog?"

"Yes." The snarky girl who lived inside her wanted to ask, *How did you guess?* But she didn't. Pissing off paying guests wouldn't cover her bills.

"I'm afraid of dogs." Nicole did an about face and fled upstairs.

"Oh, brother," muttered Celia.

She slid open the door and Lucky charged inside. Celia guessed the scent of a new person fired him up because he raced up the stairs toward the guests.

"No, Lucky," she called after him.

She grabbed a leash off the hook by the front door and raced after him. She heard a shriek and came upon the dog, who had Nicole pinned down. By the time Celia pulled Lucky away, hair and drool covered Nicole.

"Come on, buddy," Celia said, patting her thigh in the upstairs hallway. Lucky docilely obeyed, wagging his hind end. "Did you find a new friend?" she asked in a baby voice.

"Hey." Alex stepped into the hall. "Didn't she just tell you dogs frighten her?"

"Yes, she did, and I apologize," said Celia. "We just got him. I'll keep him in my apartment on the other side of the house."

"Looks like a killer, that one." A flash of humor lit up his eyes.

Celia dropped her head trying to contain herself. She was on the wrong side of customer service if she found the situation funny. But of all the dogs to fear, Lucky wasn't the one.

"I'll take him downstairs and get back to dinner."

She gave Lucky a rawhide and put him in his crate. Maybe it was nerves, she didn't know, but something wasn't sitting right about having Rob's colleagues as guests. It wasn't the clean break she needed to protect her heart.

She sent him a text.

Are you joining your friends for dinner?

His reply was instantaneous.

Yes. Should I bring wine?

Wine and Rob—a volatile mix.

I've got it handled.

Though she hadn't planned on dinner, she went all out.

Celia was in the kitchen when Alex and Nicole came downstairs, which meant Rob was a short distance away. When he knocked, her heart picked up its pace.

Alex leaned around the corner of the kitchen from the dining room. "Would you like for me to get that?" he asked, already on his way to the door.

"That would be great." She went back to working on dinner.

"Hello." Rob entered the kitchen.

Celia was bent over to check the salmon in the oven. She wanted to straighten up, but fish was delicate and easy to ruin.

"Looks good."

Is he flirting?

She straightened and faced him. Ignoring him was impossible. How could she ignore a handsome man holding a beautiful bouquet?

Slow and sexy, he whistled. "You in an apron. That's hot." He glanced at the flowers. "These are for you."

Celia didn't react to his flirting, but inside she heated to a slow boil.

"Lovely," she said. "I'll put them on the table."

"Hey." He reached out and touched her. "Is it that hard to face me?" He cupped her cheek. "What happened? Should I have not come?"

She leaned into him and let out a sigh. "Did you ask your friends to book a room and order the works?"

The question had been forming in her mind since she suspected it, but she didn't expect to blurt that out.

"Does it matter?" His thumb caressed her cheek.

"Yes, because I can't deal with liars. You could have been straight with me."

When he stepped back, his hand fell to his side. She missed his touch.

"He's here on business, and yes, I recommended your inn to them."

"But you acted surprised when they booked here."

"Is that why I haven't heard from you since our night?" His voice filled with emotion. "You found out I threw business your way?"

"It's not okay to lie to me."

"I think we have two separate issues here."

Her stomach did a flip before she felt that warm squeeze in her heart. How was it possible to be angry and yet so happy to see him?

"I'll get dinner on the table. You spend time with your friends." She pulled the salmon from the oven and plated it. "I'll come back and check on you all in a while. Usually, after I serve dinner, they are on their own and can help themselves to anything they need."

Rob stared at her while she did her best to pretend he wasn't there making her feel things she had no right to feel.

"Wow. Now who's lying?"

"Excuse me?" Her back was ruler straight.

"Don't make this about me and my friends." He leaned against the counter. "If you and I hadn't slept together, this moment would have been very different. Don't talk to me about lies when you're the biggest offender. You're not only lying to yourself, but you're lying to me. This has nothing to do with my suggesting your inn to them and everything to do with you not wanting to open up your mind, your heart, or your inn to new opportunities."

"I'm about to hit my busy season which runs from Thanksgiving to Valentine's Day. I didn't need this." The lie was acid on her tongue.

"Your guests canceled because of snow. You said so yourself, but you're going to tell me when Colorado gets its snowiest, you're booked solid?" He pushed away from the cabinet.

"Yep." She nodded. "They canceled because the snow was unexpected. It blindsided them. They were not prepared for it. Had they come here expecting snow, they would have embraced it. See how that works?"

Alex peeked in. "Are you guys coming? We're starving out here."

Celia picked up a basket of rolls and shoved them in his hands. "Here's your starter."

Alex shuffled backward into the dining room. "We can wait."

Rob continued to argue. "You're acting this way because you can't handle the fact that we slept together, and you liked it. It's not because I had someone rent out your place. Don't talk to me about lies until you're honest about how you feel about me." He looked over her shoulder to the salmon. "Dinner looks good, and I will enjoy it."

He made sure she knew their quarrel didn't rob him of his appetite.

Celia kept it together long enough to serve them dinner. She left for her apartment and went straight into the bathroom. She ran the water to muffle the sound of her sobs.

CHAPTER FOURTEEN

ROB

After the meal, Rob didn't talk to Celia. He was glad to have Alex in town because he planned to bury himself in work to take the sting out of the heartache Celia caused him. She was another woman who loathed him because he reminded her of another man. Somehow having a Y chromosome and a penis put him in the wrong.

The next morning Alex, Nicole, and Rob stood in his dining room.

"I have to run by the hardware store," he said after he and Alex looked at plans. "I'm expecting my barn any day."

Alex dropped his head, shaking it in disbelief. "I can't believe you did that for her, man,"

"It wasn't for her," Rob replied, trying to save face. "Okay, it was mostly for her." Rob and his two guests piled into his huge new truck and rolled into Pinetop.

"Nicole," Rob said. "Do me a favor. Before you go antiquing, can you walk ahead of us in the hardware store? I want to see something for myself."

Alex and Rob stayed back as Nicole wandered into the store alone. She was an attractive blonde with a Hollywood figure. Sure enough, Scott was by her side, offering his help.

"Nice," taunted Rob.

Scott looked over his shoulder like they had caught him.

"Morning, or I guess I should say, noon there, Scott," Rob gloated.

"Bobby," Scott said, flustered.

"Bobby? I'll have fun teasing you for that," murmured Alex.

"Nicole, if you want to hit the stores, there are a few a couple doors down," said Rob. "But please, hang with us."

He continued with Scott. "Did you get my calls?"

"About plowing the snow for the barn you bought?" Scott asked.

"Yes," Rob said. "Are you ignoring me, or have you been busy?"

"Not particularly busy."

"What's the deal?" he asked. "I haven't gotten a call back."

"We've discussed this. You don't have permits."

"For?" asked Rob.

"The whole harvest thing," Scott said.

"Seriously?" Rob looked at Alex and rolled his eyes. "I'm asking you to plow the snow. That's a yes or a no answer. Tell you what, never mind. I'll buy a Bobcat, or I'll get a plow attachment for my truck and do it myself. Does Pinetop pay you for snow removal?"

"Yes," Scott answered.

"Not anymore." He patted Scott's shoulder.

"I'd advise against erecting that structure," countered Scott.

"Are you a lawyer, Mr. Carson?" asked Rob. "Or the law?"

"You're a big man with your friends there, Bobby," he said, calling him his childhood name again.

Alex pointed toward the lumber and walked away.

Rob dialed the permits department which he'd saved in his contacts and put the call on speakerphone.

"Hi there, who am I speaking with?" asked Rob with tense civility.

"Margaret."

He covered the phone as though it were a landline receiver.

"Know a Margaret at town hall?" he asked.

Scott turned his back.

"I'll take that as a no," he said. "Say, Margaret, I'm calling from Pinetop. My name is Rob McKenna and I have applications for developing a piece of property. I have the permit to put up my home, and I want to erect a barnlike structure on the portion—"

She cut him off. "You're sweet with all these permit questions. Until you get approved to convert that property, you don't need a permit provided a post-construction inspection happens. Do you intend to have livestock in the structure?"

"No, the only thing I'll do is have a party," he said.

"It's the harvest festival, Margaret," Scott called out. "The Miller horse arena caved in and this hot shot bought a building so he could look like a big guy to the town and host our big event."

"Who is that?" asked Margaret.

"That's Scott Carson," Rob said.

"Scott, this is Maggie," she said. "I didn't know you were there. I would have just told him to ask you. Scott knows. You don't need a permit. Same for the fence. Did you ever get that built?"

"You know, I seem to have hit the same brick wall with that one too," he said. "Thanks for clearing that up." He ended the call and turned toward Scott. "I don't know what hair crawled up your backside, but don't screw with me like that again."

"What a tough guy, McKenna," Scott said. "Looks like Celia has a type. First Jackson Westbrook and now you. One asshole right after the other."

"I think you're upset because she skipped you. Appears she has a type of asshole she prefers, and you missed the mark," he said. "Besides the barn coming, I have a helicopter landing. I'd like the pilot to have a place to put the bird down. When can I expect the land cleared?"

Scott's jaw clenched. He seemed set off because of the news of the helicopter.

"Look, I don't know what your problem is with me," Rob said, at the end of his tolerance. He was in a bad mood because of Celia and felt burdened by the land development. He had never been one to walk away from a sound deal, but he was over it. If he hadn't invested and gotten others on board to put their money in, he would have just plunked a for sale sign in the dirt and walked away.

"I don't like the way you blow into town and have your way with one of the finest women there is," countered Scott.

Rob's brows lifted. "Yeah," he goaded. "Since you've been working on her since before I got here. Am I right? News flash, store manager, Celia and I just had a couple of dinners because I gave her son some work, and I gave them my mother's dog. There's nothing happening. Are you going to plow the snow, or do I have to talk to the owner of this place? While I tell him how unhelpful you are, I just might let it slip that you stalk every woman who steps foot in here."

"I'll send a guy out this afternoon," he grumbled.

"And if it snows between now and the time the barn or the copter arrives, I'll need that service again." Rob turned on his heel, ready to pick up a few things when he came face to face with Jackson looking at him with a bewildered expression.

"Did I hear you say there was nothing between you, my mom, and me?"

"No," Rob lied. "I mean yes but walk with me so I can explain." He headed for his designer. "Alex, this is Celia's son Jackson. Jackson, this is Alex, the guy who's creating the design for the resort we're putting in."

Jackson let him get so far and then stopped and waited for his answer. "What's going on?"

"Scott wasn't providing me with a service he should have because of my relationship with you and your mom. I had to tell him that so I could get a space cleared for the building I bought for the festival, and I guess the party after the Christmas Parade, if there is one," Rob explained.

He'd annoyed Celia because he wasn't straight with her. Lord only knew how she'd respond to him hurting her son. She could very well make sure no one came to either event since they were being held on his property.

"Jackson," he said. "You and I are friends, so I will level with you. I got caught not being straight with your mother. I went against your advice."

"What did you do?" the boy asked with concern.

"I had Alex book a room at her inn because her guests canceled, and she found out. She's not fond of me right now."

"Oh," said Jackson. "She's mad because you kept a secret?"

He knew where the kid was going with this. "It's not the same as surprising her with a Christmas present," laughed Rob.

"Right."

He'd hurt her, and that made Rob feel awful too. "I'll work it out," he promised. "I screwed up. I thought it was harmless, and it wasn't, and I should have listened to you."

"Thanks for telling me the truth," said Jackson. "Does that mean you aren't going away?"

Like his father, thought Rob. He had another epiphany. If that was what Jackson thought, then it was what Celia thought too. He'd be another man destined to leave her. While his early instinct was to hightail it out of town, he knew he couldn't. There was something much bigger than the land deal at stake. The trust of a woman was on the line and he would figure out how to earn it back.

"I'm here. I have a house and have to figure out what to do with my mother's place. I'm not going anywhere soon," he said.

"And after that?" asked Jackson.

"We're friends," he replied. "I'm up for being friends for life. Okay? What are you doing here in the middle of the day, anyway? Shouldn't you be in school?"

"I'm a junior and I have classes till the afternoon and then I go to the grocers. I'm here to get salt for the sidewalks."

"Okay," said Rob. "Are you okay? Are we okay?"

Rob was certain he'd blown it again. The last thing in the world he wanted to do was hurt that boy. As much as he should back off from Celia, he thought he should clue her in.

Nicole came back and pulled Alex in another direction through the hardware store. Rob texted Celia.

We should talk. I had a conversation with Jackson.

Within seconds, she called. As he answered the phone, he stared at the wall calendar posted at Scott's customer service station. The festival was in a little over a week, then it would be Thanksgiving, then the Christmas Parade and then Christmas. It would all happen so fast.

"This is Rob," he answered as though Celia were a business call.

"Hi, it's Celia," she said. "What happened?"

He explained, "I'm at the hardware store, and I didn't know he was here. Scott let me know I was not good enough for you, and while assuring him that there was nothing between us, and I was here on business, Jackson overheard and assumed I was leaving."

"What did you say to him?" she asked.

"I told him I had no problem being friends for life, and I meant it. I wanted to let you know, so it didn't seem like I was hiding anything, and so you could make sure he's okay," he said.

"I'll find him. He should be at work by now," she said. "Thanks for telling me."

"I care," he said. "We're having a late lunch at the counter, and I'll take care of dinner for Alex and Nicole, so you don't have to worry about them."

The Pinetop Drugstore still had a lunch counter, and if it was still like he remembered it with hand-mixed shakes and an amazing menu, he'd be happy. He needed a meatloaf sandwich and some roasted tomato soup.

"Hey, let's go eat," he called to his friends, who were checking out the ornament display.

On his way out he told Scott, "I have your number." It was more of a threat than a reminder.

"I'll clear it today," the disgruntled man said.

Rob was on edge. Being so close to Celia and not being able to have her was like sitting in front of a plate of chocolate cake and not being allowed to eat it. Since he'd had a taste, all he wanted was more.

"I can't wait to get this project started," he said to his guests.

"I just got a great idea about the motif of the resort," said Alex.

"Good," he said. "Talk to me at lunch. I need comfort food."

CELIA

The temperatures in Pinetop were fickle. The snow from earlier that week receded fast as the temperatures climbed higher than normal. Thanksgiving was around the corner, but it didn't feel like it with afternoons reaching the mid-sixties.

Apologizing was all Celia could think of. She owed one to Alex, Nicole, and Rob.

Rob was right. She'd been dishonest with him and with herself. History repeating itself had paralyzed her from experiencing the wonder of him—of them.

She broke out her special guest picnic basket and loaded it with a fresh cranberry tart, a thermos of coffee, a loaf of French bread and artisanal cheeses. She'd checked out the wine Rob had in his house the night they had dinner. His selection was far better than hers, so she didn't include a bottle.

Nothing she packed in the basket would turn back the clock and let her start over. She was at fault and had to clear things up between them. While he wasn't honest, he was thoughtful. At what point had she considered him sending business her way a problem? He wouldn't tell her because he was trying to protect her fragile ego. *I'm such an idiot.*

She changed into a pair of jeans, a cashmere turtleneck, and her good Timberlines. She whipped her hair back into a wispy braid and spritzed on her softest perfume. When she saw Rob, she wanted him to look at her like he had that night they made love.

She put the basket in the front seat. After she stopped by the market to make sure Jackson was okay, she would track him down. Pinetop wasn't too big that he could get lost forever.

She put Lucky on his leash and let him sit in the backseat of her car. Jackson had been spending a lot of time alone in his room and she hoped the pup would snap him out of whatever was going on.

Once parked, she called him. As soon as he appeared, Lucky went nuts. Celia wondered how Fiona had handled him the way she did. Despite his size, he wedged between the seats, and before she could save it, put his paw through the picnic basket lid.

"No!"

She got out of the car and bolted to the passenger's side to get him off the basket. Her apology food was ruined, and her heart was in her stomach. To make matters worse, when she opened the door, Lucky pushed past her and went straight to Jackson, who tried to grab hold of him.

Two elderly people left the drugstore and Lucky charged toward them. They pressed against the brick building and he went right into the open door. Jackson ran forward, but Rob appeared, leading the dog outside as if this was an everyday occurrence.

Celia approached the seniors to ask if they were okay. "I'm so sorry." Tears pooled in her eyes.

"We're fine, dear. That jolt was better than a cup of coffee," said a white-haired woman she didn't recognize.

"Mom," said Jackson. "Mom." He stooped so they were eye to eye. "Are you crying?"

Celia took a deep breath and tried to hide her emotions.

"I got a little upset." She swiped at her eyes before a tear could fall. "I thought the dog would mow those ladies over for sure."

She worked up the nerve to look at Rob. It wasn't as if she hadn't seen him the other day, but in the daylight, with the bright blue Colorado sky for a backdrop, he was gorgeous.

"Hey," she said. "I had something to give your friends since they aren't eating at the inn, but I think Lucky might have ruined it."

"What is it?" he asked.

"It's in the front seat." She frowned as she made her way to the passenger door. A little spark of hope flickered in her. Maybe the enormous animal had not put his huge paw in the food and mushed it to oblivion.

"I gotta get back, Mom," Jackson told her.

"I brought Lucky to make you smile," she laughed.

"Goal accomplished." He kissed her cheek and took off toward the grocery store.

When she replayed the whole fiasco in her head, she laughed. Celia couldn't control herself. She leaned against the car and let go. At some point, she started to sob. A hand rubbed her back.

"Hey," Rob whispered. "Hey." He drew her into his arms. In front of the shopping center, he held her like he owned her.

Her heart would not argue. She pressed her face into his steely shoulder and let him comfort her.

He looked at Lucky and the pulverized basket, then shook his head. He whispered in Celia's ear, "It will be okay." The stress in her body melted away. "I'll hold the dog," he said. "Check out the damage."

Celia backed away, wiping her eyes and her nose. She opened the door and inspected the contents. She gasped and smiled at the same time.

"I don't believe it! He must have gone right between everything. The tart's a little crushed on the edge, but the rest looks okay."

"You packed us a picnic basket?"

"Yes. I was bringing you guys lunch." She stopped herself before she cried again.

"Shh ..." he soothed her. "You know what this means, don't you?"

"What?"

"This means you have to eat with us," he said. "Take the basket out of the car and put it in the trunk, and then let's roll the window down for Lucky," he directed.

Celia hurried around to the driver's side and followed his instructions.

"You want me to join you guys after everything I've done?" She sucked in a shaky breath. "I'm so embarrassed."

"I'll help you get over that." He moved in front of her. "I'm getting the site for the festival cleared. The structure is on its way. By next week it will be like there had always been a barn there. And you know what else?"

"What?" she whispered and wrapped her arms around the small of his back.

"Alex and I will survey the property by helicopter." Men became boys when anyone mentioned helicopters. "After we take care of business, would you like to go for a spin?"

She nodded. At this point, she'd go anywhere he asked.

"You know who else would like that?" He looked over his shoulder to the grocery store. "Jackson."

"Yes, he would."

"Come on." He opened the door and Lucky jumped inside to take his place in the back seat.

"You left your friends at the counter," Celia reminded him.

He looked adorable when his face was awash with surprise.

"Oh, yeah, you're right."

Celia clicked her key fob to lock her car. "We'll be right back, boy."

Rob led her into the drugstore, holding her hand. She didn't want to let it go. She was embarrassed about the mild tantrum she'd had at dinner, but with Rob there, she had the courage to show her face. When they got to the counter, Nicole and Alex were halfway through their meals.

"We're going to check out the second-hand stores after this," said Alex. "Nice to see you, Celia."

"You too."

They sat on the stools next to Alex and Nicole. Rob put his arm around her as they read the menu together.

"I know what I want." He looked straight at her. "But I can't have that here."

She looked up at him. "I think I do too."

He looked at her. "Are you sure? I want you to be certain this is what you want."

"I'm sure." She knew they were talking about more than a meal and glad they were being honest with each other.

"There's plenty of time to make a choice."

"I choose you, and because of that choice, I have to trust you," she said.

"I won't let you down."

"Now what are you going to have for lunch?" she asked.

"Meatloaf sandwich. I'm happy to see they haven't changed the menu since I left." He ran his finger down the offerings. "It's literally the same."

"Maybe. Then again, some things got better with age." She leaned into him.

Alex looked at Rob. "You two good?"

"Yes, we're good, but she's nervous about the resort." Rob pressed a kiss to her cheek.

"Why?" Alex asked. "It will be great."

She knew it would be great. Great for everyone but her. She also knew that progress was inevitable, and she'd have to get used to change. "You guys will put in gift shops, fancy rooms, and a spa." She swallowed hard. "Who wants to stay at the inn when the resort will have everything I don't?"

Alex nodded. He knew she was right, but it wouldn't stop him from designing the place.

"Be honest," she asked Nicole. "If you had a choice between my place and a plush hotel which would you choose?"

"I'm not sure. I like your place for a day or two, but a hotel would be great long term," she said.

Celia tried not to make a face. "Thank you. That was honest." It served her right for asking the question. Now she was nervous, but she didn't want to let it ruin the moment. She did a quick accounting of her blessings and at the top of the list was Rob still liked her, and the basket of food only looked destroyed but wasn't.

"Take the truck." Rob pulled out his keys and handed them to Alex. "I'll drive back with Celia and Lucky."

"The dog?" asked Nicole with alarm.

"Yes. The dog. Big furry beast that will lick you to death." Rob waved to them. "See you later. Helicopter mañana."

Finally, they were alone. Rob leaned in and kissed her. "I've been craving that for days."

"Me too," she said into his mouth. "Me too."

CHAPTER SIXTEEN

ROB

The next day Rob munched on the loaf of bread and cheese Celia had packed and watched the flatbeds with the prefab barn pull onto his land. They had arrived much sooner than expected, making the rush to get them erected less stressful.

Just beyond his house was a helicopter and a swarm of big rigs loaded with the skeleton of what would house the harvest festival. Rob made sure that Jackson was present so he could see everything come together. A bonus was that with Jackson came Celia.

"We will build the resort with structures like these," he explained. "I have them built to order and we put them together where we want them. Instant development."

"Won't they fall apart?" Jackson asked.

"They snap together, but they'll stand as long as your mother's place. In many ways, they're more structurally sound. These prefab buildings are fantastic. If I had a barn built on-site, it would have taken me at least a month. This ... I can buy them online and have them shipped. Once all the pieces are in place, it doesn't take the crew much time to put it together."

"Sweet," said Jackson.

Rob looked over his shoulder at Celia, soaking in their conversation. Everything about her seemed relaxed.

"After I take Alex and your mom up in the copter, I'll take you up and show you the property."

"Can Lucky come?" Jackson asked.

"Jackson, my boy," said Rob with a grin. "You are a hard kid to say no to, but um, no. You can hang out here if you like while we're up in the air or go inside the house and help yourself to the fridge." At the mention of food, Jackson set out on a run to the house.

The helicopter was a four-seater. Rob pressed his hand at the small of Celia's back and helped her inside.

"Are you nervous?" he yelled over the whoosh of the blades rotating above their heads.

"Yes, a little," she said. "But I'm good."

"Yes, you are good. Very good," he flirted.

They put on their headsets so the pilot could communicate with them.

"You look hot," he murmured.

"Why, thank you," Alex responded.

Rob's eyes widened.

Alex laughed. "I can hear everything you say, so either shut it down or titillate me."

Celia's face turned crimson.

Rob wrapped her petite frame in his arms and gave her a bear hug.

"Sorry," he whispered.

They took their places in the helicopter and lifted off. They looked at one another with alarmed expressions as the big bird banked right. The nerves passed and Rob was about to narrate when he caught the look on Celia's face. She leaned into the window and watched as the land below them sped by.

"Like it?" he asked her.

"It's breathtaking," she said. "No wonder your mother did nothing with it."

"Nothing is the keyword. We never visited it. Talked about it. Zilch. And she never got to see it like you're seeing it now."

"If she had, she would have known what an absolute treasure she owned." The view mesmerized Celia.

Rob continued. "See right there," he said to Alex, pointing at an opening in a copse of trees. "That's where I want to put the main watering hole, slash casino, slash nightlife spot. Right there up against the mountain rise. Beside it would be equipment rentals and maybe the ice-skating rink. I can re-purpose the barn for that. The lodging can be on roads leading in and out like a racetrack. Jogging and bike lanes, the whole shot."

Alex snapped shots of the land with his camera.

"We can go closer to the mountains if we need to," said Rob.

"I'm fine," replied Alex. "I think I got the critical areas."

Celia spoke up. "Won't there be a traffic problem if you have the bar next to the rentals? Shouldn't you have them spaced out?"

Rob paused because he thought that was an excellent point. He looked to Alex, who slumped at Celia's statement of the obvious.

"Yes and no," said Alex. "Then you have people annoyed when they return their rentals and have to trudge to another location to have their cocktails."

"Provide a shuttle," she blurted.

Rob arched his brow.

"Well, yeah," said Alex dejectedly. "That would work."

"Don't worry," Rob said to Alex with a laugh. "You still have a job."

Celia was quiet.

"What else are you thinking?" he asked.

Her shoulders slumped. "Just what a shame it is to wreck this amazing land. It's beautiful."

He understood her position. She worried that construction would destroy the natural beauty of the land.

"Sweetheart, it's been here since I was born, and until I moved back, I'd never seen it. I don't think anyone in

Pinetop has either. It just exists. Isn't it time we shared it with everyone?"

"Are you saying it's a waste?" she asked.

"One sec," he said to her. "Alex, have you seen what you need to see?"

"Yep," he said. "I have some good ideas, including Celia's."

"Okay," Rob said to the pilot. "We can go back. We'll do that second tour I told you about."

The pilot nodded and turned the craft. Rob could feel Celia's mood change.

"What about the wildlife that depends on this land?" she asked.

"I'll be respectful to the environment," he promised. "I was thinking of putting a presentation together to show residents at the harvest festival since they're setting up a stage, anyway."

"You mean for the Pinetop's Got Talent show?" she asked.

He and Alex and the pilot chuckled.

"Yes," said Rob.

"But then it would turn the harvest tradition into a business meeting."

"Business *is* coming to Pinetop, Celia. It came here before. That's how Pinetop started, and it's coming again." He hated how they were taking one step forward and two steps back. What Celia needed was a change, but she would fight him every step of the way. What she didn't realize was he was a worthy opponent. Her ex might have cut tail and run. In some ways, he had done the same. When he was young, he didn't like the way his life was turning out, so he abandoned it for a different one. In her mind, she couldn't see the one thing that would make him stay was her.

"Pinetop isn't in survivor mode," she said. "It's not like it's going anywhere if you don't develop the land. You're doing it to make money and move on."

Fortunately, the flight was fast, and the helicopter's arrival back at the field changed the subject. As it descended to its landing spot, his stomach took a free-fall drop which he suspected was true for Celia as well because she stopped talking.

"Are you still okay with Jackson taking a spin?" he asked.

"Yes."

"I'll be right back, and we can talk."

"No, it's okay," she said. "I'll be fine."

"Oh no," he said. "We're having a talk."

She unbuckled herself and followed him into the house to collect Jackson.

"I'll watch the dog," she said.

"Why don't you join us?" Rob asked. "I think it would be a nice thing to experience it together."

Rob guided the dog to his spare room. "Off you go, Lucky buddy," he said. "Come on, Jackson, let's take your mom for a ride."

Rob suspected Celia would be quiet through the ride, but he wasn't about to let her get away with it. He helped Jackson with his headset and pointed out things on the way.

"Hey, can we do a flip?" Jackson asked the pilot.

Celia braced against Rob.

"No," she protested.

Rob and Jackson laughed. The pilot grinned and shook his head.

"I think we're good to go," said Rob to the pilot, who then turned and headed back to the house.

Celia was lighter after the second trip. By the time they landed, the progress on erecting the barn was remarkable. They'd hoisted one side into place by cranes.

"Wow!" exclaimed Jackson.

"Exciting, isn't it?" Rob said.

"Is this what you do?" asked Jackson.

"I rarely get involved in the actual building part like I am now. I cut deals. But in this case, I'm wearing all the hats. Neat, huh?"

"I know what I want to do when I grow up," he announced with a huge smile. "I want to be Rob."

Rob laughed. "There are worse things." He led them to a table filled with food for the crew. "Let's eat. A man can't live on bread and cheese and tarts alone."

Jackson piled his plate high, but Celia's was empty.

"Aren't you going to have anything?" Rob asked.

"Sure," she mumbled.

He still felt like she was sulking.

"What's going on?" he asked.

"Just lots to think about."

"This happens when people come into our lives. Things change," he said with a whisper.

"I love this," Jackson yelled over the noise.

Celia and Rob both turned to check out the boy's plate piled eight inches high with food.

"That is some sandwich you got there. You going to finish that?" Rob asked, knowing the answer already.

"No problem," Jackson replied with a smile.

"Someone's happy," murmured Rob into Celia's ear.

"Yes," she said. "I see that. Be patient with me."

"Like I said," he whispered. "We'll talk."

Alex and Nicole appeared.

"Hey man," he said. "I think I have everything I need. I'll send my ideas to you once I get home. We're heading out."

Rob stood up and shook hands with Alex.

"Nicole didn't get a copter ride," Rob said.

"No thanks," Nicole laughed. "I like helicopters less than I like dogs. I prefer my feet on the ground."

"Me too." Celia tapped her foot on the solid ground.

"We were thinking of coming back," said Alex. "We want to come to the party once the barn is up and wondered if we could have our room back?"

Celia looked up, first to Rob and then to Alex.

Rob shook his head. "That's all him. I had nothing to do with it."

"We like your place," Alex said. "We like Pinetop, and I figured if I hope to design something that blends in, I have to know a little more about the town."

"I'll look at the schedule, but I can work something out for sure." Celia shook Alex's hand and gave Nicole a quick hug. "Thank you for putting up with me."

"Change is hard, but you've got Rob, and he'll make it easier." Nicole pulled Alex toward their rental.

Rob looked at Celia. "She's right. You have me."

The crew chief in charge of building stepped up and helped himself to food.

"How's it going out there?" Rob asked.

"Great. It will take another day or so to put together and inspect, then she's yours."

"Not bad," Jackson piped in.

Rob would have thought he was talking about the food if Jackson wasn't looking straight at him.

"These buildings are great, Jackson. I can take this down and move it if I want. And I save a ton on labor and other costs," Rob said.

"Are you sure they're not flimsy?" Jackson asked the crew chief as if he didn't believe what Rob had told him before.

He pointed to the barn. "That baby is solid as they come."

"It's a 'baby'?" muttered Celia.

"Hey," Rob chastised.

"Teasing," she said.

If she'd have to adjust to all the changes he was imposing, he figured he could cut her a break. Everything had happened in a rush. A fabulous and delicious rush.

"Teasing is good," he said.

"Okay," said Jackson with a grin. "I'll leave you two love-birds alone and walk my dog."

"Are we lovebirds?" asked Rob.

"I don't know," she said.

He led her away from everyone. "I know I just got here, but I think we could have something special. That first night we made love, you jumped in with both feet. I'd like to see you do that again. Take a leap of faith, Celia. We have something worth exploring. I'm willing to go at your pace, but you have to talk to me. What do they say to kids? Use your words?"

"It's the land, not you and me."

"Are you sure that's it?" he challenged.

"Yes. It was very moving to see how majestic it is, and now it will be—"

"Fabulous." He kissed her on the forehead, interrupting her. "You have to risk something sometime, sweetheart. You need to trust someone; why not give me a chance to prove to you I'm worthy of your trust? I want to love you like you deserve to be loved, but I won't pressure you anymore." He tossed his full plate into a nearby trash can. "I'll leave the ball in your court."

CHAPTER SEVENTEEN

CELIA

When the barn was put together, it looked wonderful. It wasn't seasoned like the Millers' horse arena, but spacious and clean. All the members of the harvest festival committee appreciated having a place to hold the event.

The committee, including Scott, put up the stage. One volunteer set up the sound and the microphones for the talent show. It was brilliant and yet bittersweet.

Rob saving the day would charm the townsfolk. He would introduce his resort plans to the people at the festival. They might fall in love with him or just the opposite. She was on both sides of that fence. When she was near him, her heart felt full, but when he talked about the development, she thought she would lose her mind because the success of his business meant the end of hers.

It was such a generous move to buy the barn, but she knew it wasn't altruistic. The barn would gain him favor. The town of Pinetop didn't understand how fast Rob McKenna could move, both in his personal life and his business life. Was it possible to love a man and hate him at the same time? She would have to come to terms with the inevitable. She had to pick her battles. If she fought the resort, she could lose Rob, and that wasn't an option. Her heart was all in when it came to him.

THIS WAS IT. The festival was upon them. Celia dressed in a cream colored wool dress and a jean jacket paired with boots. It was like she was going to a high school dance and hoped Rob would like what he saw.

She called Jackson on the intercom, intending to put a fire under his butt. They had to go now, or they'd be late.

"Hey, where are you?" she asked. "Are you ready to go?"

He didn't answer. She looked out front for his truck and found it gone so she called him.

"Already here," he said. "I'm in the show. Surprise. Lucky and I are doing a number."

It floored her. Tears of pride stung her eyes.

"Really? Why didn't you tell me?"

"Did you not hear the word surprise?"

"No, I heard it. Just can't believe it. I can't wait to see you."

She pulled out of her driveway and headed toward Rob's. A touch of loneliness filled her as she drove. He'd offered to come and get her, but that seemed counterproductive. As she neared, she saw the spotlights around his place. She remembered them fondly. When they were in bed, the silvery lights outlined him. The image of his naked body emblazoned in her memory forever.

The last few days had been busy for both of them. Him building the barn, and her getting the inn ready for the holidays. She took a moment to say a prayer and count her blessings so she could temper her excitement. She had the strongest urge to talk to him but knew he was busy. Instead, she sent a text.

I'm on my way and parking in your driveway.

With Jackson performing, she wanted to park close and get inside to save a front-row seat.

Parking was one detail they had not thought of when moving the festival.

Cars parked in the field, but she swung by the front of his house. It wouldn't hurt if she parked on the street or in his driveway and cut through the house.

When she opened the storm door and found the front door locked, she rounded the house and made her way to where the crowd was gathered.

Over her shoulder, she saw Scott pull his truck beside her car. He had the same idea to avoid the chaos by parking in front. She hurried around to the back, trying to avoid him. Lately, everything with Scott was a confrontation, and she didn't need the stress tonight. She hadn't spoken to him since he'd cashed her check.

He rushed forward until he was a few steps behind her, though he said nothing. He shadowed her like a stalker.

Moments later, he spoke. "What's the matter? Didn't Romeo give you a key?"

She didn't acknowledge him, just kept moving.

"Yep," he said. "Jackson Westbrook all over again. Men like them take what they want and leave the rest behind for men like me to piece back together."

Celia was practically running now. Up ahead she saw a familiar face. "Hey, Alex," she said.

"Evening, Celia. I thought we'd stop here first then head to your place after."

"Great. The key is under the mat."

Scott stormed beyond them toward the arena.

Alex noticed the hostility. "Are you okay?"

"I am now," she said. "Can you walk me the rest of the way to the festival?"

"Sure thing. Rob is already there. He's setting up to give his presentation. He'll introduce me, but I'm waiting for Nicole. We can all go together. How's that?" The couple had returned for the festival because Rob thought it wise to have Alex around to field questions.

Scott got yards ahead before relief washed over her.

"I think I'll go ahead," she said. "Thanks, anyway. Tell Nicole I said hello."

She walked slowly enough to stay behind Scott so she could watch him. If he went left into the barn, she would go right.

"Hey, Celia," said Dave Swanson from her side. "There are a couple of spots on the end if you want to go around."

They packed the place. Rob walked onto the small stage and took the microphone out of the stand. He stepped off to the side of a large white piece of canvas hung to use as a screen. It was time to talk about business. Celia was nervous for him but interested in seeing him in action.

He looked handsome in a crewneck sweater with a button-down tucked underneath. Because he was tall and good looking, he had an appealing presence. She took a seat and with her chin resting on her fists, she listened. One glance to her right, and she saw Scott staring at her. Her instinct was to roll her eyes, but she ignored him. She'd learned long ago not to poke a bear.

"Good evening, everyone. I'm Rob McKenna. I grew up here in Pinetop. You might have known my mother Fiona, who passed away recently. Her internal drill sergeant would have whipped this into shape with ease." The crowd chuckled. "I'm glad to be a part of this tradition, but before we show off our local talent, I want to share a brief presentation I put together about plans for the land we're on." He stepped aside and pointed to the screen. "Enjoy."

The lights went down, and the soft murmurs turned into silence.

Rob set his presentation in motion while he narrated.

Celia loved his voice but wanted to turn away from the pictures that would mean her backyard would become a megaplex with asphalt and mud and trash, but that wasn't what she saw.

"At first, we went a different route, but the town inspired my designer Alex Brandt. We also had some strong input from Celia Roberts. We borrowed from a community in Carmel, California where they tried to blend the structures into the natural setting as much as possible. I think we've done a good job merging the old with the new. While we have strived to maintain most of the natural beauty of the land, with the town's permission, and only if you want this, we would like to feature your businesses as an added selling point. We don't want to create competition but bring prosperity to the town."

Rob flipped through the remaining pictures, allowing them to speak for themselves. They were beautiful. The buildings weren't modern designs, but a mix of the architecture already found in Pinetop. Rob had taken his prefab, mix and match ideas and made them work so the resort blended with the town. Decked out with the natural flora, they appeared to grow from the landscape. It overwhelmed her. She couldn't express her gratitude because the Pinetop's Got Talent show would start right after the presentation.

"Thanks for watching, and now, on with the show. Our first act is Lucky and his boy Jackson Roberts," said Rob.

No one sat behind her, so she stood to get the best view. The crew did a much better job with the lighting than she expected. Her sweet son, carrying his guitar and leading Lucky on a leash, sat center stage on a stool Rob set out for him. Lucky lay at his feet, and the crowd said a collective "Aww."

"Rob mentioned his mom, and I would like to acknowledge mine." Jackson stared straight at her. "I'd like to dedicate this song to Celia Roberts, who is the best mom a kid could have." He settled the guitar in his lap and began to strum.

It floored her to see him playing the guitar effortlessly. Where had he been hiding that talent? Jackson shared a lot, but there was so much she didn't know about him. She assumed he played videos all the time when he'd been practicing.

He sang a song about his hero and that was her. She felt a presence behind her and for a second, she thought she saw a ghost from her past, but as the person moved into the light, she realized it was Rob.

Her emotions had played a trick on her. Despite Scott's accusation, Rob and Jackson Sr. were not the same man. Rob had proven he could compromise. He took her wants and needs into consideration. To this man, she mattered. She threw her arms around him and without thinking, shouted, "I think I love you."

"Right on, Mom," said Jackson without missing a beat and continued singing.

The audience roared with laughter and then erupted into applause. Celia and Rob did their best to contain themselves so Jackson could finish his song. She turned around to face her son and pressed her back against Rob's chest. When the song was over, they walked hand in hand outside.

"It's surprising Lucky isn't freaking out," said Rob.

"I can't believe my son can play the guitar."

Jackson had left the stage and dashed around the barn to Celia, who took her son's face in her hands.

"I had no idea," she said.

"I know," Jackson said. "Not all secrets are bad. It's your Christmas present, but when I learned this was a show, I went for it."

"I'm so impressed, and it was beautiful."

"I heard you loved it," he teased. "Oh, I mean you love him."

"I love you both," she said.

"We should go back and watch the show," Rob suggested.

"I want to put Lucky in your house," said Jackson. "He gets antsy around too many people."

"I'll let you in." Rob pressed his hands above Celia's hips, steadying her for a kiss. "Save me a seat."

Rob's and Jackson's voices faded into the distance. Her heart filled with joy. Life was just about perfect.

CHAPTER EIGHTEEN

ROB

Thanksgiving was a thing of beauty with Celia cooking a feast for the three of them. They had the standard meal of turkey with all the fixings, from stuffing to cranberry sauce. He couldn't remember the last time he'd had a feast of that magnitude. His mother never celebrated the holiday, and he wondered if it was because she wasn't thankful.

After their food settled, Celia pulled down her artificial Douglas fir from the attic. Rob and Jackson carried boxes of ornaments and lights and spent the evening turning the Hummingbird Inn into a Christmas inn.

By the time they finished hanging hundreds of bulbs and yards of tinsel, there wasn't much of the tree to see.

"What's the point of having a tree if you can't see it?" He sat on the sofa looking at the masterpiece before him. His mom always had a tree, but it was because she liked the way it looked in the window when people passed.

There was never a time when he raced from his bed on Christmas morning and found a mound of presents waiting.

He was certain that only happened in the movies.

Not that Fiona didn't celebrate the season. The first week of December, she had him sit at the kitchen table and make a list of things he needed.

Like Jesus, he got three gifts. One was always a package of socks. Another was underwear, and the third was a surprise. The best gift was when he opened a small box and found a set of keys. They were to a used SUV. It wasn't a gift for him but for his mother, so she didn't have to drive him places any longer.

On graduation day, he drove out of Pinetop and never looked back. When the lawyer read the will, he knew he couldn't ignore his legacy. It was more than the land, more than the house. It was his way of turning nothing into something.

Celia curled up beside him and tucked herself under his arm. "Does the tree bring back memories?"

He looked at Jackson, who sat on the floor and admired the ornaments.

"Yes, some bad and some good." He'd put off the not so fun stuff for long enough. Tomorrow he had to face his past. "While I know I need to close many chapters, starting with my mom's house, I'm making new memories with you and Jackson." Celia was his sanctuary. Though she was part of his past, she was also his future.

They sat for more than an hour staring at the twinkling lights and admiring the ornaments Celia had collected over a lifetime.

"I should go. Tomorrow will be a busy day." He didn't look forward to walking into his childhood home.

"Would you like me to go with you?" Celia asked.

Jackson hopped to his feet. "I could go too."

Rob unraveled himself from Celia. "I think you have to work, young man." He turned to Celia. "I don't want to take you from your business, but if you're free, I can use your wise counsel. I have a Victorian that needs repurposing."

HE'D DRIVEN by his mother's house which, aside from a housekeeper entering to dust and vacuum once a month, had remained locked up. There was no doubt he had avoided the house in the same way he had avoided his mother for all those years. They didn't have the relationship Celia and Jackson did. He realized now that he was responsible for that too.

He left the engine idling when he exited to knock on Celia's door.

Celia answered, looking pretty as ever. She wasn't the girl he'd had a crush on in high school. She was the beautiful woman he loved now. He stood and stared at her.

"What?" She rubbed under her eyes. "You have a strange look on your face. Is my mascara running?"

He wanted to give her those three words, but he hesitated because they required perfect timing. He could have told her at the festival, but he didn't want to take her moment of spontaneity away and overshadow it with his own proclamation of affection. He wouldn't wait long, but he would make it special. Celia deserved more than what she had.

"No, you look beautiful. I never tire of seeing you."

"Wait until I'm eighty." Her eyes grew wide as if she hadn't considered them growing old together.

"I'll still want you when you're eighty. Now let's go." He stepped aside to let her out. "You want to drive the Jaguar?"

"You'd let me?"

"Anything you want, sweetheart."

He raced after her to the car. She was inside and buckled up before he could say another word.

She didn't wait until he fastened his seatbelt before she drove off. Her enthusiasm filled him with happiness and fear.

Was it wise to let Celia loose with all that horsepower at her fingertips?

"I think it's shorter if we cut through the streets closer to your house," he said, pointing at the one they passed.

A smile lifted her lips. "I know, but I want everyone to see me. I've got a hot man and a hot car."

He looked out the window and thanked the universe for bringing Celia Roberts into his life. "Have at it then. You can drive as long as you want. In fact, if you want this car you can have it," he said.

She turned and gawked, taking her eyes off of the road.

"Watch out," he said with a touch of panic in his voice.

She snapped her head forward and turned sharply, over-compensating, and stopping.

"Maybe I shouldn't drive." She gripped the steering wheel with white knuckles. "It might be too much car for me. You might be too much man for me."

"Nope on both counts. This car and I were made for you."

"You're very generous." She licked her lips, reminding him of how generous she'd been the night before.

"I've done well in business but not so well with personal relationships—until now. Until you. You've given me every-thing." He looked at her. "I'd give you anything to make you happy."

"What more could I want?"

He thought of a few things he wanted to give her but now was not the time. "Eyes up front, missy."

They drove to his childhood home, which was an authentic Victorian like Celia's, but unlike hers, it was poorly maintained.

He noted as they passed, the other houses were decked out for the holidays like the Hummingbird Inn, but his mother's house looked like an unkempt orphan. It was a sad house in need of attention. That's why he'd avoided it. As soon as he was able, he'd paroled himself from the misery. It was the prison where Fiona McKenna had served her time.

As they got out of the car, it filled Rob with emotion. The most prevalent was guilt. Had he let his mother down or had she let him down? He didn't know the answer to that question.

Celia was the one who brought him out of those morose thoughts. She held his hand as he pushed through the gate of the weathered picket fence.

"Wow." He swallowed a boulder-sized lump stuck in his throat. "This is a little more emotional than I expected."

She touched his shoulder. "I'm here for you."

He took the keys and unlocked the door.

"I pay the light bills," he said as he flipped the switch. "I have a person come in and clean the place."

Everything was as she'd left it. Nothing had changed since he'd lived there. Every stick of furniture was in its place. One or two things were covered with sheets, but it was the same.

"Time warp," he said.

"It's beautiful," Celia remarked. "Very sweet." She moved to a decorative table in the corner and picked up a picture of him as a baby. "I don't remember you ever being this small. When did you come to Pinetop?"

He remembered the exact day they'd pulled up. "I was seven and my mother moved here in search of independence. She had it until the townsfolk found out she'd never married." In some ways, he was just like his mother because he'd left for his independence.

She moved around the room. "It's a beautiful home. Needs lots of work, but we could bring it back to its original beauty."

"You like everything of my mother's. First her land and now her house," he joked.

"No, I like her son first. The rest is just stuff. Means very little without you here."

"What should we do with it?" he asked. "I have a place and so do you." He faced her. "I meant what I said about not competing with another business. What if you converted this to another inn and ran them both? Could you do that?"

She looked at him strangely.

"Have I grown a third eye?" he asked.

"Are you giving me this house too?" she asked.

He shrugged. "What am I going to do with it? If I kept it as an inn, then I would be in direct competition with you. Or I could pay you to manage it—"

She put a finger to his lips. "You're keeping the house?"

"Yes, I think so." How could he erase his past when it had brought him back to Pinetop and given him Celia? "I didn't know until now."

"Okay, then we have to do the house proud," she said. "We have the Christmas Parade in ten days. It's a tradition that's been around for decades. Don't you remember it?"

"I do." He'd never gotten into the floats or decorating for the parade, but he remembered how the town rallied around the holiday. It was as if every resident dressed their house up for Sunday dinner.

"Isn't it time this house saw happiness?" She spun around in a circle, taking in the parlor. "We can decorate it for the parade. I have some extra stuff. I'll bet your mother has a cache of decorations stored somewhere. This could be fun."

She squeezed his hand, making him feel raw with sentiment. It was hard to feel anything but joy around her. She was the embodiment of Christmas.

"That's a great idea." He considered his mother, who had been abandoned by the man she loved. "I think she would want it to be happy."

"You're probably right."

"Did you know her well?" he asked.

"Enough to say hello when she came to town. She was always with a dog and enjoyed eating at the lunch counter."

He nodded. "I should have come home sooner, but she treated me like a job. She fed me, clothed me, and raised me. When I grew up, she was done." He brushed a hand over his face. "I flew her out a couple times to see me, but not much changed. She was critical and aloof, and always compared me to my father. My mom raised me to be nothing like him, so the comparisons were painful."

"Did you ever see him after he left you?"

He walked through the living room skimming his fingers across the dark burled wood furniture.

"I never met him when I was young. But once, when I was developing some land in Arizona, I walked off the site and a man came up to me and said he thought I was his son."

He yanked the sheet off the floral settee his mother always sat on. If he closed his eyes, he could see her there knitting doilies.

"What did you say?"

He shook his head to dislodge the memory. "I told him I had no father and walked away." It was a bittersweet memory in his life. "I had projects that took me all over the place, but I could have come back. I should have. This is a big house. Too big to live in alone."

"You don't need to be alone," she said with a soft smile.

He looked down at her and didn't see an accomplice to the bully who used to torment him, but a woman who loved him.

He led her to the settee and helped her take a seat while he took a knee. "Celia, will you marry me?" The words fell out of his mouth without thought.

"Why don't we focus on getting this place together, warming it up, and getting it ready for the Christmas Parade for now?" she said. "We can talk about the other later."

It felt like their roles were reversed. Now Celia was the calm one.

"You're right. I was impulsive and didn't think things through. You deserve better than what I just gave you."

She leaned over and kissed him. "Let's look for decorations."

"Are you changing the subject?"

She moved her lips across his.

He didn't push it for now. She didn't say no, and his inner voice was giving him clear direction. He needed to make it special and that had to start with telling her he loved her first.

CHAPTER NINETEEN

CELIA

Celia and Rob climbed to the attic where they suspected Fiona stored seasonal stuff. Opening the box of Christmas decorations was like opening a time capsule. Rob's mother had what Celia thought was the coolest collection of vintage ornaments, but he barely remembered them.

"Oh, my gosh." She held several in her hands. "These are wonderful."

"I forgot about this stuff." He touched a strand of packed bubble lights.

He looked through other boxes and paused at a velveteen box he held on to.

"What's that?" she asked.

"Just some stuff that used to sit on my mom's dresser years ago. I'll look through it later." He set it aside.

She dug through the boxes. Each item she unwrapped became her new favorite treasure. "This will be the best-decorated house in Pinetop." She bounced with excitement.

They put up every decoration, opting to create an interior window display in honor of Fiona. They had probably once used some ornaments outside, but they were too precious for that now.

"This old-time Santa and Mrs. Claus will be such a hit." She burst with excitement.

After examining one cord and finding it frayed, her shoulders slumped.

"We can still set it out, but it would be cool if it lit up."

"Don't give up yet," he said. "Let's go to the hardware store and see if they have a replacement. I can try to switch it out."

They took a break for lunch and to look for lights.

"I want to get a flocked artificial tree for the window." She could see it now, the white tree lit with colored lights. She hadn't been this excited in a long time.

"Whatever you want. This is your baby, but we need my truck if you want to get one today."

"Scott should be able to deliver one."

"Not if I'm with you."

"This is a small town, and he knows better than to push the envelope that far." It had been over a week since she saw Scott. She had mixed feelings about the man. Half was disgust and half disappointment. Neither would garner kindness.

Celia drove the Jaguar to the front of the hardware store. She wanted to run the errands first and then have lunch at the counter. A sudden burst of enthusiasm took over when they approached the entrance.

"We have to hurry because I'm dying to plug in those lawn ornaments."

"Have I spawned a new obsession?" He snaked his arm around her waist.

"I'm all about Christmas. That should have been obvious last night when we decorated." She smiled as her insides heated. He had asked her to marry him, something she needed to think over when she was alone.

She stopped short and when he collided with her, she stumbled, but he caught her just as they stepped on the sensor to open the sliding doors. Scott, sitting at his customer service station, turned around and scowled.

"Afternoon, Scott," Celia said with happiness in her voice.

Rob's hand was on her stomach. Hers covered his as they shuffled into the store.

Scott turned back to his work.

"If I bought an artificial tree, would you deliver it to Fiona McKenna's address?" she asked.

"I'd have to charge a fee. Bobby could pay for it."

Celia knew he was trying to goad Rob by calling him his high school nickname, but neither of them gave him the pleasure of reacting.

"How much?" she asked.

"You know what?" Rob said. "We'll buy rope and tie the tree to the top of the Jag. It's only a few blocks." He stared at Scott. "Thanks anyway."

He hurried Celia away from the customer service desk.

"You'd risk that paint job because he's a jerk?"

"Yes, I would," he said. "We can buy a mover's blanket, or I'll get a piece of cardboard."

"Or we could get your truck or borrow Jackson's. Come on. I know little about fancy cars, but I have paint job intuition. We're not scratching that car."

Rob stopped like it inspired him.

"Do you think Jackson would like to drive the Jag home? We can switch keys?"

Celia wasn't on board. There was no way she'd put that much power in her son's hands. "No way. Jackson is not driving that car."

"Just a thought." He shrugged. "One day then. Maybe for the prom or homecoming?"

Celia melted. "You like my son, don't you?"

"I do." His hand went to his heart. "He reminds me of me, only I didn't have you for a mom. Mine wasn't so intent on making me happy."

Celia's throat tightened as emotion welled within her.

"You're a good man and not your mother or father. The man you are is perfect for me," she whispered.

"I'm glad we're on the same page."

"As parents, we do our best. It's not always good enough, but it's all we have in our toolbox at the time. I wasn't perfect for Jackson. Despite my influence, he's his own person. He'd rather eat a burger than a salad. He stays up too late. I have to remind him at least twice to do his chores, but I love him." She covered her heart with her hand. "I still can't get over his performance at the festival. Where did that come from?"

"He got that from you." Rob leaned forward and kissed her.

"Ahem." Scott cleared his throat.

Rob whipped around and cut his eyes to Scott.

Celia took his hand and tugged him toward the door. "You can take Jackson out for a spin during broad daylight on a flat, paved surface. In the meantime, let's go next door and borrow his truck." She bounced on the balls of her feet. "Let's get the tree and decorate for Christmas."

"I wish there was another place where we could get a tree." He looked past her to the door. "I don't suppose you would go for cutting down a real one and painting it white?"

"No way. I like the fake ones because it leaves the real ones alone. The sooner we get the keys and load up, the sooner we can go home and have grown-up fun."

"What kind of fun did you have in mind?" he said loud enough for Scott to hear.

Celia knew Scott had his eye on them and heard everything.

"Rob," Celia warned. "Let it go."

"Sorry," he said and kissed her again.

They picked up what they needed, grabbed carryout from the counter, and went back to Fiona's house to set up the tree.

"We have to do your house next." She could see it now. A huge tree next to the wall of glass decorated with hundreds of glass balls and strands of popcorn and cranberries.

"I don't think my house is on the parade route, sweetheart."

"We can do it for you and for me."

There was an unexpected knock on Fiona's door. Rob and Celia glanced at each other.

"No one knows we're here but Jackson and Scott." Rob answered the door to find Dave Swanson on the porch. "Hi there, Mr. Swanson. It's good to see you again."

"Afternoon, Mr. McKenna."

"Please call me Rob." He opened the door wider and stepped aside. "Won't you come in?"

The old man was reluctant, but accepted Rob's invitation.

"Afternoon, Celia." He looked around the parlor. "I see you're decorating Fiona's house."

"It needs it." She clutched Santa to her chest. "Look at these. Rob and I plugged them in and only one works." She pointed to the other. "Poor Mrs. Claus needs a new plug to be ready for the Christmas Parade."

"About that," he said. "I got a complaint, well—um." He shoved his hands in his pocket and looked at the ground. "Saw the truck outside and thought I'd nip it in the bud."

"Is there a problem? What can I help with?"

"Well, the problem is the two of you."

The sting of a thousand bees pierced her heart. "There's no problem." She set Santa down and moved to stand by Rob.

"Folks have complained about public displays of affection verging on pornographic. It's not becoming to a member of our Christmas committee. As the president of the committee, I have to address all complaints." The poor man's face turned cherry tomato red.

"Was this complaint lodged by Scott Carson by chance?" Rob asked.

"Yes," said Dave. "And he said he would withhold his help with materials including the trailers if you stayed on the committee. Without those, we can't complete our floats."

"He's jealous," Rob growled. "And you can't undo the work she's already put in. The parade is almost here. If it weren't for Celia, I wouldn't have remembered about the Christmas Parade or known about the festival. Let's not forget I bought a barn so we could have the festival. It's the same barn where we'll hold the party after the parade."

At the reminder, Dave shook his head.

"Jealous, huh? I could see that," Dave said with a wink toward Celia. "I delivered the message, but don't believe it. Wish I could tell him if he doesn't want to be on the committee with you then he can take himself off, but the hardware store donates the trailers that haul the floats. He can't fire you from the committee, but he can refuse to provide the trailers. It would be a shame to give up the parade because of jealousy. Lots of people have worked hard to make it what it is."

"Celia is one of those people," Rob said.

"And so is Jackson," she added. "He goes to school and works at the grocery store and helps everyone out in his free time." She tried hard not to cry, but she needed to.

"I need to give Jackson his truck back," she said. "Thanks for stopping by, Dave." Her stomach flipped and flopped. She thought she might be sick. She heard the message loud and clear. If she stayed on the committee, then there wouldn't be a parade. She wasn't stepping down. Some things were worth fighting for and tradition was one.

"I'm sorry, Celia," Dave said.

"Don't be. I'm not letting Scott Scrooge ruin Christmas." She spun around to leave. "Mr. Carson and I are going to have a talk."

Rob touched her arm. "Wait a minute."

"What?" she snapped back.

"I don't want another second to pass without telling you something," he said. "Before you walk out that door feeling like you failed or that you're not good enough, I want you to know that I love you, and you're perfect for me."

Her heart did a triple flip. He was such a good man. "I love you back." She fell into his hug.

"Go get him," said Dave. "Do you mind if I take Mrs. Claus back to my house? I have a way with the older ladies." He laughed. "A little touch here and there and I'll get her working again."

CHAPTER TWENTY

ROB

Rob wanted to rage at Scott but there wasn't a place for that approach in Pinetop. He drove Jackson's truck back into town but gave Celia space to figure out what she would say. While it was in his nature to step in, he knew this was something she needed to take care of herself.

"Not a word to Jackson," she said as they parked.

She dropped off the keys and together they went into the hardware store. Rob stood by her side and listened. The one piece of wisdom his mother gave him was that women didn't want rescuing, they wanted someone to hear them.

"Scott." She moved toward him like a charging rhinoceros. "How dare you?"

He had nothing to say. He could no more stand his ground against the beautiful Celia than Rob could have.

She stood in front of him and poked his chest with her finger. "I've been nothing but kind to you. Jackson left us—"

Her voice cracked, and she regained herself. "And I have waited a long time for happiness. My son and I deserve it." She pointed to Rob. "I'm going to marry this man because damn it … he makes me happy."

Rob grinned. He tried to contain his joy, but he couldn't.

"If you're mad at me, then talk to me about it, but do not punish the entire town because you're having a childish moment. You're not a toddler. You're a man. Act like one."

"He's …" Scott started.

"Who I want," she finished. "Now apologize," she ordered.

Scott huffed and rolled his eyes but did as she demanded.

"I'm sorry, Celia," he said. "It's just …"

"No justs. It's time to be the guy I know you to be. A generous man who has a lot to offer someone other than me."

"You're right, but you're a hard one to let go," he said.

"You can't let go of something you never had. Let's be friends. You wouldn't want me to be your enemy."

He nodded. "Friends."

"The Christmas Parade is on as planned, right? No more threats?" she asked.

"No." He lowered his head like a kid in time out. "No more threats." He looked at Rob and shook his head. "You're one lucky bastard."

"That I am," he said, and held his hand out to shake. Part of him didn't want to sweep the harassment under the rug, but as a resident of Pinetop, he had to let it go. He came out the victor. Celia had chosen him. The last time he'd felt this accomplished was the first time he'd completed a multimillion-dollar deal. That achievement didn't make him feel all warm and fuzzy inside. It didn't make his heart feel full enough to burst. He'd been chasing deals all his life to fill the void left by an unhappy childhood. Funny how he had to come back to the one place he'd sworn off to find his future.

Celia turned to him. "Can I drive the Jag home?"

Rob laughed. "Anything you want."

He expected her to drive back to his mom's house, but she drove to the inn. He followed her lead because it felt like she had a plan. She put the car in park and made her way to the front door. With her hand in his, she led him through the common area and to a door off the kitchen. Once there, she flipped a switch and lit an apartment that looked like they'd built it in the 1950s. Remodeled or newer construction, but not Victorian.

"This is your place?" he asked.

"Yes," she said. "I think someone with money owned the house. That's why I thought this would make a perfect inn. It has accommodations for a staff and stuff. The mother-in-law suite out back is like this too. I believe at one time a huge team operated this house."

"And you do it all by yourself." He admired her for so many things but mostly for her resilience and never give up attitude.

"Jackson helps."

"I know." He was in love and Jackson was part of that equation. While he would have been in love with Celia regardless, having Jackson around just made it sweeter. "I can't say it enough—he's a great kid."

"That warms my heart to hear that," she whispered. "He needs a good role model."

She slipped her hand behind his head and drew him in for a kiss.

He remembered something and abruptly broke away.

"Wait," he insisted in an urgent whisper and dashed back to the entryway for his coat.

He pulled out something he'd discovered in the attic. In the box that rested on his mother's dresser for years was his grandmother's wedding ring.

He carried it back to her, hoping she liked it, or they could figure out how to make it theirs. The ring was platinum, that much he knew. The stones looked like diamonds but who knew? What he liked was the story behind the ring.

His grandfather had ridden a horse for a hundred miles to get back to his grandmother Charlotte after the war. He'd traded his prize horse for the ring and traveled the last fifty miles on foot. It proved that a good woman was worth the sacrifice. He'd give up everything for Celia if he had to. She was worth more than a horse.

Rob got to the threshold of her apartment and paused. His hands shook. He proposed and told her he loved her at moments that were less than romantic. Sucking in a deep breath, he approached her and dropped to his knee.

"Celia." Emotion threatened to take his words.

She beamed down at him as Rob offered her the ring.

"I know this is fast, but I'm a fatalist and believe the gift of the land was my mother's way of calling me home to be with you and Jackson. The second I laid eyes on you was the first day of the rest of my life."

He'd never given marriage a thought. Never envisioned what he would do if he proposed, but as he balanced on one knee, tears trailed from the corners of his eyes.

"Will you take this ring as a symbol of my love and commitment?" He slipped it on the edge of her finger. "I want to be by your side forever, if you'll have me. I'll be a good husband and a good father to Jackson. I'll be proud of him for the man he is with no expectation of who he should be."

"Oh, Rob." She looked down at the vintage ring. "This is beautiful."

He knew her well enough to know she meant it.

"You have the same expression as when you came across my mom's lawn ornaments," he said. "Is that a yes?"

"Yes," she replied with a nod.

He rose, letting his hands feel the backs of her thighs on his way up. The sweet, firm curve of her backside filled his palms before he moved his hands north to cup her face and kiss her.

"I like this proposal stuff," she whispered.

"It gets better," he promised in a husky tone.

He lifted her until she wrapped her arms and legs around his waist and walked with her toward her bedroom.

"This way?"

"Uh-huh." She tucked her head into the crook of his neck and breathed him in.

"I love you more than you'll ever imagine, Celia."

"I can imagine a lot."

"I love you a lot." He set her down on the mattress.

"You know what?" She rubbed her hand over the soft duvet. "No man's been in my room since my ex left."

He swept her hair from her face and kissed her before stepping away to undress. They held one another's eyes as they took off their clothes.

When Celia stripped down to her bra and panties, she moved back on her bed and offered herself to him. Through passion-heavy lids, she unhooked her bra and slipped off her panties.

The world moved in slow motion as they made love. In an instant nothing else mattered but Celia, her pleasure, and her happiness.

As she peaked, he slowed the pace to make the moment last. He made love to her until the afternoon turned into early evening. Sated and in love, they soaked in a bubble bath in Celia's claw-footed tub.

"So, future Mrs. McKenna," he said. "We have a fake Victorian with a barn, your lovely inn with this great apartment—"

"Our lovely inn," she corrected him with a sweet smile.

"Our lovely inn," he amended. "And my mom's house. Plus, a resort in the making. What do you think?"

"It's a lot," she said. "I like your mom's house."

"And I'm loving this tub," he said. "We fit wonderfully in it."

"We do." She relaxed against his chest and sank deeper into the bubbles. "At first thought, we could run the resort as a business, run the inn as a business, and fix up your mom's place to live in."

"You enjoy fixing up stuff, don't you?" He rubbed a soapy sponge down the center of her chest.

"I think I like it better than the customer end of the inn."

"Alex and Nicole like it here," he said. "I could rent the fake Victorian to them. And then there's Jackson. He may stay on in town after he graduates. Maybe he'd like to have one of these places."

"We are not giving our son a house for high school graduation."

"Too much? What about the Jaguar?"

She turned her head to look up at him. "You know it's not what you give us that makes us love you, right?"

He held her chin in place. "Yes, it is. I give you my love."

She giggled. "You're right, and it's the most valuable gift I've ever received."

He pulled her against his chest so she could hear that his heart beat for her.

CHAPTER TWENTY-ONE

CELIA

The Pinetop Christmas Parade started at one end of town and followed a path through the residential areas until they came out on the other side. The floats were lined up while folks in costumes waited to board them. Dave Swanson was the official Santa Claus and would ride in the last float and pass out candy to the children who waited on the sidewalks.

Celia had never figured out what she wanted to do for her float. Her mind was so full of Rob that nothing came to her. She stood on the curb and watched everyone take their places. This year she'd be one of hundreds of spectators, and that was okay.

Looking for Rob and Jackson, she walked through the dozens of floats until she came upon one that said Christmas Inn Love.

"Why hadn't I thought of that?"

Lucky came out of nowhere, tugging Jackson behind him. "Mom, do you love it?"

"I do, but whose is it?"

Rob stepped out from behind the wooden cutout painted like an inn. Her inn. He moved through the flocked shrubbery placed to mimic real foliage.

"It's yours." He offered his hand and pulled her up to take one rocker on the fake front porch. Jackson and Lucky joined them.

"You built this for me?"

Rob shook his head. "You built this. All of it." He spread his arms and turned around. "How did you think the Christmas Parade could do without you?"

"It has every year. I've never had a float in my life."

"Time for new traditions, Mom," Jackson said.

She looked at the sign swinging from the eave of the porch. "It's so spot on I might have to rename the inn." Without it, she would have never been in Rob's path. The inn had been her savior. Looking at the two men in her life, she realized she had more than a person deserved, but she wasn't complaining about anything except for the weather.

The air was crisp and cold with a storm coming in. She rubbed her arms and shivered.

"Got you covered." Rob pulled a blanket and a thermos of hot chocolate from a nearby bag.

She wrapped it around her shoulders. Small-town values surrounded her. There was hard work, family and friends, commitment, simplicity, support, tradition, and teamwork, but nothing was better than love. Love of family, love of self.

Love of Jackson and Lucky and Rob. Love was the core of all things good.

"I'm not dressed for Christmas." She glanced down at her jeans and boots. "I could have dressed as an elf or a cobbler if you'd told me."

"Cherry or apple?" Jackson asked.

"Haha." She laughed. "You're thinking about your stomach."

"I'm a growing boy."

Rob patted him on the back before he took the other rocker. "You're a young man, and I'm proud of who you're becoming." They sat in chairs with Jackson and Lucky on the floor below them.

"Shall we tell him?" Celia asked Rob.

"That I'm not buying him a car for Christmas?" he joked.

Celia playfully socked him. "No, silly. *Tell him*, tell him," she hinted.

They had agreed to wait on telling Jackson about their engagement until the ring was adjusted and back on her finger. They wanted the moment to be special for all of them.

"Love is our theme," she said looking down at her son. "To me family is love." She held out her engagement ring for Jackson to see. "You, me, Rob, and Lucky are a family."

Rob looked to Jackson, hoping for his approval.

"You're getting married?" His voice cracked as each word rose an octave.

"Are you okay with that, buddy?" Rob asked. "I would ask you for your permission and everything, but I opened my big mouth and asked her first."

Jackson turned his head and Celia knew he was about to cry.

She was fearful that she had made a mistake in telling him this way, or that maybe he liked Rob, but she should have run the decision by him first. But when Jackson lunged forward and threw his arms around Rob in a big hug, she knew they'd done the right thing. The three of them embraced.

"My fiancé loves prefab, and this is perfect, but who did the design?" Between her and the resort, Rob didn't have a free moment, so someone had to help.

Alex stuck his head outside the cab of the truck. "We're moving. Are you ready?"

"You." She pointed at him. "You designed this?"

He shrugged. "It was a group project."

Having a designer around was quite a boon. She held Rob's hand as the parade began and their float lurched forward. Above them, the *Christmas Inn Love* sign swung back and forth. It wasn't only a pitch for her inn but a declaration of their love.

Celia looked down at where Jackson had taken a seat with Lucky. "Do you think he'll be okay while we're moving?"

"Yeah, I brought lots of treats," Jackson said.

"So did I." Rob reached into the bag and came out with boxes of cookies and bags of chips. "These are for humans." He ruffled Lucky's fur. "But we'll share."

"That's what families do," Jackson said as the float made its way down Main Street.

The weather held as the caravan progressed from town through the residential areas.

"Look," Celia said to Jackson. "That's Rob's mom's house. And look …" She nearly flew off her rocker. "Mr. Swanson fixed Mrs. Claus."

Even though it was twilight, the lights on Fiona McKenna's house were lit, including the vintage lawn ornaments they'd dug out of the attic. She looked at her ring as she laced her fingers with Rob's. "I love you," she said.

"I love you," he replied. He turned to Jackson. "I love you too, son."

"If I call you Dad, do I get to drive the Jaguar?"

Rob laughed. "See, sweetheart? We don't have to give it to him. He just wants to borrow it."

"Wait, what?" Jackson almost fell off the float, but Rob reached forward and grabbed him before he toppled off the side.

"Let's make it through Christmas, and we'll see what the new year brings," Celia said.

Jackson reached into his back pocket and pulled out a piece of paper and a pen.

"What are you doing?" Celia asked.

"I've never had a father. I'm making a bucket list." He turned to Rob. "Do you play ball? Camp? Skydive?"

"No, but I've been practicing that video game."

Jackson hopped up and nearly climbed into Rob's lap. "You'll be the best dad ever."

Rob held both Celia's and Jackson's hands.

"I don't know what being a good father or husband looks like, but I'll do my best to be fair, to be honest, and to put you both first."

"Mom, where did you find him?"

Celia giggled. "On our front porch."

CHAPTER TWENTY-TWO

ROB - ONE YEAR LATER

A lot had happened that year. Nicole bought the Hummingbird Inn. She and Alex moved into the connecting apartment the day Celia, Jackson, and he moved into their new home. This was their first holiday together as a family.

When Rob raced down the stairs on Christmas morning, what he saw in front of him was more than he had a right to ask for. His life had come full circle. The house that had brought him so much pain was now a place of joy.

"Sweetheart, I told you I'd feed her."

Celia looked at their baby girl and smiled. "Why should you get all the fun?"

Behind them, Jackson took the steps two at a time with Lucky hot on his heels. "Did Santa come?"

He might have been seventeen, but at Christmas, he would always remain a child.

Celia had a rule. If you didn't believe in Santa, the tree would be empty on Christmas morning.

"Looks like Santa was good to us this year." Celia cradled their newborn in her arms.

Jackson looked at his little sister who had been due Christmas Day but came two weeks early. "I wanted a brother." Last year on the float, he'd made a list of things he wanted to do and have. At the top was a sibling.

"You weren't specific enough," Rob teased.

"I will be next Christmas."

"Next Christmas?" Celia asked. "You're already putting in requests?"

"Yes, I love my little sister, but I want a brother. I know nothing about girls."

Rob knuckled his head. "You've got a mom."

"Yeah, but she's not really a girl."

Rob laughed. "Oh, son, you've got a lot to learn."

Celia handed baby Holly to him. He stared into his little girl's eyes and fell in love all over again.

They broke ground on the resort and got married on the first day of spring. That night they celebrated new beginnings. Little did they know baby Holly's life had begun then too.

"What did you put on your list?" Jackson asked.

For a man who had once counted on three things for Christmas in his youth, he hadn't asked for anything.

"I refused to tempt fate by asking for more than I already have. This year I hit a trifecta. I got a wife. I got a son. I got a daughter. What more could I want?"

Jackson stared at Rob. "What about a new Jaguar so I can have your old one?"

Rob took a seat next to Celia.

"Jackson my son, look around you. What do you see?" Rob looked around his childhood home. They'd brought it back to its full splendor. He saw more than the walls, the flooring, the trim. If there was one thing he could teach Jackson, it was the lesson he hadn't learned until he met Celia.

"I see a bunch of presents that need opening. A baby who needs to eat. A dog who'd rather be running in the snow than sitting in the house."

"At your age, I would have seen the same." He took in his surroundings. "You know what I see?" It wasn't the paint, or the refinished wood floors that made it different. It was his perspective. "Everything changes with love. I see hope, happiness. I see my family and my future."

"Guess what I see?" Celia asked.

Jackson looked at the tree behind them. "A big January credit card bill?"

"No." She shook her head. "I see a long-standing tradition forming. My husband, my children, our pets will surround the tree. There will be carols and cookies and candy canes, but more importantly, there will always be love."

Jackson handed out the gifts and as a tribute to his mother, Rob made sure everyone got the prerequisite socks and underwear. Lucky got a jumbo marrow bone.

He was rich, very rich, but it wasn't the millions in his bank account that made him so. It was the love of a woman who shared not only her son but her heart. Happiness wasn't found in things, but in the people who brought richness to his life.

GET A FREE BOOK.

Go to www.authorkellycollins.com

NEED MORE HOLIDAY HAPPINESS?

ABOUT THE AUTHOR

International bestselling author of more than thirty novels, Kelly Collins writes with the intention of keeping the love alive. Always a romantic, she blends real-life events with her vivid imagination to create characters and stories that lovers of contemporary romance, new adult, and romantic suspense will return to again and again.

For More Information
www.authorkellycollins.com
kelly@authorkellycollins.com

www.ingramcontent.com/pod-product-compliance
Lightning Source LLC
Chambersburg PA
CBHW070502200726
48293CB00007B/2333